Helen Frindle's working life has been eclectic but always included creative activities, particularly art, which led in mid-life to her enrolling for a BA (Hons) Fine Art Degree.

She came to live in South West France 2005 and experienced a complete change of circumstance. Creative activity had to take second place. Despite this, discovering the history of the local region and her interest in alternative theories of human spiritual evolution she rekindled her creativity by writing her first novel.

The Mists of Memory is the author's second novel and the sequel to the *Sentient Shield*.

Now settled in France, Helen continues to paint and write.

This book is dedicated to Gillian Doward.

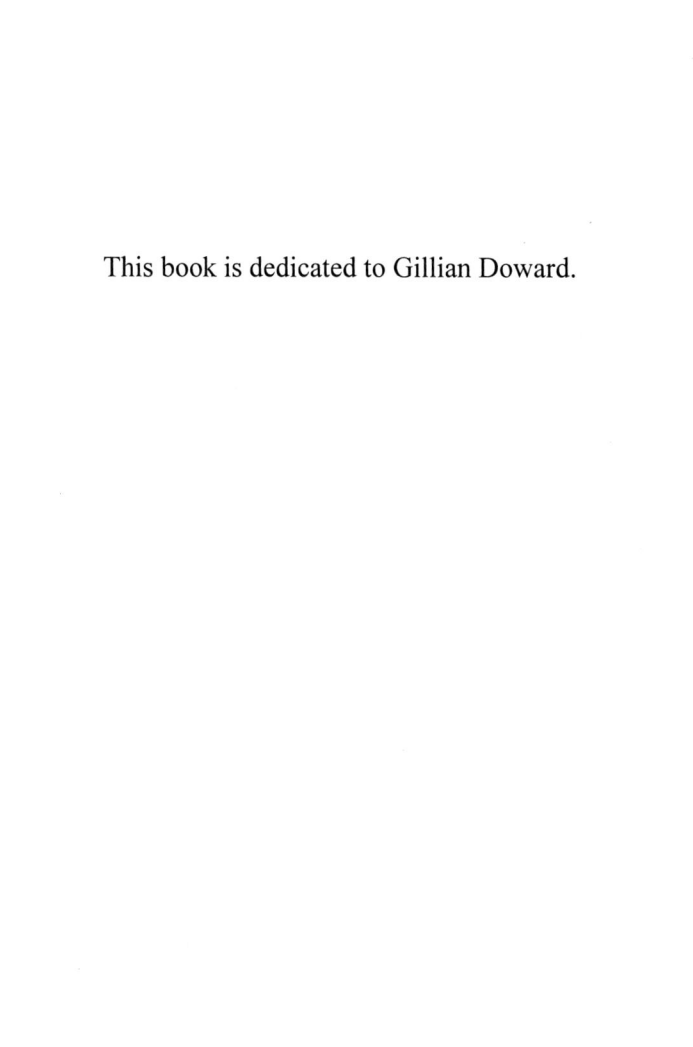

Helen Frindle

THE MISTS OF MEMORY

AUSTIN MACAULEY PUBLISHERS™
LONDON • CAMBRIDGE • NEW YORK • SHARJAH

Copyright © Helen Frindle 2023

The right of Helen Frindle to be identified as author of this work has been asserted by the author in accordance with sections 77 and 78 of the Copyright, Designs and Patents Act 1988.

All rights reserved. No part of this publication may be reproduced, stored in a retrieval system, or transmitted in any form or by any means, electronic, mechanical, photocopying, recording, or otherwise, without the prior permission of the publishers.

Any person who commits any unauthorised act in relation to this publication may be liable to criminal prosecution and civil claims for damages.

This is a work of fiction. Names, characters, businesses, places, events, locales, and incidents are either the products of the author's imagination or used in a fictitious manner. Any resemblance to actual persons, living or dead, or actual events is purely coincidental.

A CIP catalogue record for this title is available from the British Library.

ISBN 9781398486805 (Paperback)
ISBN 9781398486812 (ePub e-book)

www.austinmacauley.com

First Published 2023
Austin Macauley Publishers Ltd®
1 Canada Square
Canary Wharf
London
E14 5AA

I would like to thank the following people:
Gillian Doward for her continuing faith in me as an author and for the inspiration she has given me.
Roger Evans, for his love, support and encouragement.
Austin Macauley Publishers.

Table of Contents

Preface	**13**
Part I	**15**
Chapter 1: Grace	*17*
Chapter 2: Maddy	*26*
Chapter 3: Maddy Meets Magda	*33*
Chapter 4: Maddy Visits Nammu	*41*
Chapter 5: Nammu Reviews	*46*
Chapter 6: Return of the Halqu	*54*
Chapter 7: Philippa	*59*
Part II	**65**
Chapter 8: The Medici Lineage	*67*
Chapter 9: Return to France	*78*
Chapter 10: Maddy Meets Grace at the 'Croft'	*83*
Chapter 11: Granny Madeleine	*94*
Chapter 12: Family History	*100*
Chapter 13: Grandfather Jack's Notes	*104*

Chapter 14: Return to the Venus POD	*114*
Chapter 15: Vaxchtajn and Lord Andrews	*119*
Chapter 16: The Weekend Break	*126*
Chapter 17: Maddy Reflects and has an Encounter	*142*
Chapter 18: Nammu and Malachi Ponder	*145*
Chapter 19: Ring of Fire and Sleeping Giants	*149*
Chapter 20: Philippa Panics	*152*
Chapter 21: Maddy Explains to Grace	*160*
Chapter 22: Evacuation	*164*
Chapter 23: Reconnecting with Pam and the Lightworkers	*175*
Chapter 24: Nammu and the Meeting Place	*180*
Chapter 25: The Gathering	*183*
Chapter 26: Departure	*190*
Chapter 27: Arrival on Essassani	*192*
Chapter 28: The Halqu	*196*
Chapter 29: Finally, Now, Waiting	*199*
Appendix I: Preface to *The Sentient Shield* Helen Frindle (2018)	**201**
Appendix II	**210**
Footnotes and References	**212**

The Croft nestled into the side of the valley high in the Pyrenees. The air was still and clear and conveyed a sense of anticipation.

The occupant of the Croft sat staring out across the valleys, her body gently moving in and out of density, visibility. Her thoughts were with what she had been through in this incarnation on this planet Earth. An ancient guardian of the universe she had held the Seal of planetary protection for aeons. Feeling aged and weary in this three-dimensional existence, she knew it was time to relinquish this presence and ascend; to face reawakening her soul to its place in the Universal consciousness.

The Alignment had passed and Earth had been given the opportunity to ascend. The Halqu, vanquished, had disappeared.

The tsunamis were approaching. Moving to the doorway of the Croft she saw the waters rising in the distance. This world she had inhabited was about to be swept clean and to restart with the help of the ancients. The fate of its inhabitants was gravely in question – would they survive or die in the waters? Those Earthlings selected by her mentors had been transported to a holding planet to observe Earth's fate. She was aware that those chosen by the Halqu had also been removed by star-ships.

The ancient guardians watching over the universes had tried many times to set Earth on an evolutionary path in line with the rest of the harmonic universe within which it existed. From its birth millions of years ago the planet had observed many civilisations existing on its surface. Some lived in symbiosis with the planet and evolved naturally, others were created by visitors from distant star systems. In all cases they created, flourished and then died. Some civilisations resulted in extinction events after which the planet started afresh.

The ancient guardians watching over these evolutionary experiences were frustrated. Earth should have developed to what it was destined to be, an example of harmonic evolution, a library of all the elements that exist in the Universe moving back to Source, the ultimate explanation of existence. In Earth's more recent history it had been evolving well, everything was proceeding naturally but then visitors arrived in the latest period, that of Pisces, threatening the population's potential.

The visitors came with purpose to plunder the planet for gold, a much-needed element for the survival of their own planet. In doing so they created a civilisation on Earth that had endured to the present day, the twenty-first-century. Other visitors, notably the Halqu, also arrived with a far more threatening goal. Their interference resulted in the crisis concerning the Alignment and in addition further exacerbated the climate change Earth was already experiencing.

Is Earth going to ascend or descend? Dimensionally the options were open.

The woman turned from the doorway and stepping up through the dimensions took her place amongst the ancient guardians to stand and observe.

Preface

Although *The Mists of Memory* is the sequel to *The Sentient Shield*, it can be read with ease and enjoyment without having read the first novel whose storyline concerned a journey towards an event called the Alignment – a specific time in Earth's history when Earth played a pivotal part in the evolution of the Universe. At the point of Alignment, Earth would ascend to a higher dimension, that is from a three-dimensional existence, 3D, through 4D to 5D, ascension being a higher level of spiritual and emotional development. This ascension depended on Earth and importantly the spiritual awareness of its population at that time as to whether this could be achieved.

Maddy is the central character and as a symbol she represents the awakening of spiritual consciousness and of the ultimate goal of returning to Source. In her many incarnations over 8500 years to the present day she has carried her family lineage as part of her role as protector of Earth's future.

The Halqu are the extra-terrestrial visitors to Earth and have pursued Maddy through time, especially during the thirteenth century when the Alignment opened portals to time/space/dimensional travel. Having destroyed their own planet the Halqu needed to access the portals so that they could return to their home planet at an earlier time with the aim of revising its evolution. This was the reason behind their persistent pursuit of Maddy.

As a *Sentient Seal* part of *The Sentient Shield* Maddy achieved her goal allowing the Alignment to take place and the Halqu to be defeated. The question then was; would Earth ascend or descend?

Malachi and Isolde, also extra-terrestrials, were assigned to Maddy to assist her during her journey. They were appointed by Overseer Fraterne Nammu, an ancient guardian who appears at intervals in comically quaint apparel. In the *Mists of Memory* it is these three who alert her that something was amiss and that the Halqu might be returning and that they might be manipulating Earth's fate.

Two incarnations have particular relevance to Maddy's quest; in the thirteenth century during the Cathar Inquisition and later in the sixteenth century and the rise of Protestantism in Europe. Both periods of time show Maddy's family relationships and the human characters become vivid participants woven into her quest. In addition to Maddy's identity and role as carrier of the line she is very recognisable as a wife and mother.

In the *Mists of Memory*, Maddy relinquishes her present 3D incarnation in the twenty-first century and returns to her soul existence, that of an ancient guardian of the universe. In the unfolding of events we see Maddy, and the ancient guardians, observe an extinction event on Earth. Maddy and her present family along with a percentage of the Earth's population relocated to a planet in a faraway galaxy and Earth being cleansed by water and fire.

The fate of the planet and its population is in jeopardy.

Part I

Time present and time past
Are both perhaps present in time future
And time future contained in time past,
If all time is eternally present
All time is unredeemable.
What might have been is an abstraction
Remaining a perpetual possibility
Only in a world of speculation.
What might have been and what has been
Point to one end, which is always present.
Footfalls echo in the memory
Down the passage which we did not take
Towards the door we never opened
Into the rose-garden. My words echo
Thus, in your mind.

Four Quartets,
Burnt Norton, 1
T. S. Eliot

Chapter 1
Grace

(England 2013)

Grace had been worried for some time about her mother who had not contacted her recently. It was two weeks now and there had been no phone call – usually they would speak to each other at least three times a week. Nobody else seemed to be worried or taking her concern seriously.

Richard, her husband, had left for work early and she had dropped Jonah, their son, off at school shortly afterwards. Grace now sat, a mug of steaming coffee in front of her, mulling over the situation. Up until now she had only spoken to close family, Richard, her father, Colin and David, one of her brothers who lived close by. Her other brother Mark was travelling in Asia, currently in Cambodia.

They had listened, but had been, she thought, dismissive, her father especially. This had annoyed her because he had said that since her mother had settled in France she had become increasingly vague, strange, hippy-ish! What kind of expression was that? He had further commented on how she was dressing very differently.

It had made her really cross remembering how her mother had only gone out to France in the first place and reluctantly due to her father's encouragement. All of this seemed to her now to have been to get her mother out of the way so he could carry on with the woman who was now her stepmother. She could feel herself becoming angry and decided it wasn't helping. She really needed to find out whether her mother was safe and coping.

Grace Madeleine Zagel Williams was 40 years old and lived with Richard, her husband, and Jonah, their only child, in a small village in Hertfordshire. She had two brothers, David and Mark (Jameson), and was the youngest of the siblings. Her parents, Maddy and Colin (Jameson), and grandmother, Madeleine Gill, all originated in that same area.

In her early life she had been brought up in London; she and her brothers had led a city life and then attended university. Grace married Richard, a fellow student, and when they decided to settle down it had suited them both to move close to Grace's family roots.

Richard was an aeronautical engineer working at nearby London Stansted Airport and Grace had worked as a legal secretary in a local solicitors' office until Jonah arrived. Since then she had become involved in local voluntary charity work, the hours fitting in around Jonah's schooling and extra-curricular activities.

Grace had grown up in a very close and loving family. Life was good but for some few months she had become increasingly concerned about her mother. She and her mother had been close, that is until her mother went to live in France a few years previously. Her mother had retired at the same time as her father. Her mother had been a teacher in London, her father a stock broker in the city.

After retiring her parents had settled into comfortable routines. Her father played golf and her mother loved the country life and her garden, having had only a small paved courtyard in their London house.

Grace's first inklings of concern arose when her father had returned from what her mother called a 'jolly' with his friends. This had led to her parents' buying a house in the Pyrenees on the French/Spanish border. The first thoughts of Grace and Richard when they heard about it were, *wonderful, we can have some lovely holidays*. It sounded very beautiful, idyllic, high up in the mountains, clear air but remote.

Initially she realised her mother was not keen and she had confided to Grace that she had felt pushed into it. She also shared that she was angry with Colin as she had thought they were quite happy as they were. And then there was this house in the Pyrenees. However, her mother sent by her father with her old friend Helen for company, had visited the house and had returned seemingly enthusiastic about the idea.

Her parents went out in the first couple of years every two to three months for long weekends and two week summer holidays. During that time they had set it up. In the spring of the third year they had both decided to try an extended stay. Grace had gathered the family together to send them off. Arriving for the party, however, there had seemed to have been some altercation between her parents. It transpired that her father had not renewed his passport and therefore couldn't travel out with Maddy to start their stay.

Following that, her father instead of joining her mother, had become involved with a project run by an ex-colleague. Eventually there had been a confrontation and her mother discovered that he had been having an affair. Subsequently her parents separated and Grace's mother stayed on in France to sell the house. Her father went to live with Diana who was now Grace's step mother. She was a nice enough woman but it had caused the whole family to step back and resulted in some estrangement between Grace, her brothers and the family in general with their father.

Her mother stayed in France and did not sell the house. She liked it there and had settled, perhaps because it was far away from the situation. The cause of Grace's current concern was that she seemed to have disappeared. Grace did not know what to do. Her thoughts were that she should go to France and try and find out what had happened to her mother. She was in a good position to do so as Jonah, their son, was now 17 years old and thinking of his further education. In addition she had plenty of help from her grandmother, Madeleine, who was the only person as concerned as she was.

First things first, she would discuss the situation with them and speak to her father and get his reaction to the situation.

-◇-

Colin was having a bad day. Having retired several years previously he was beginning to wonder what he was doing. He had got involved in a project with an ex-colleague and friend, Chris.

Now Diana had left him. He was beginning to see how much Maddy, his ex-wife, had put up with. He had drifted into the relationship with Diana and initially it had woken him up and made him feel alive. He hadn't realised how much of a rut he and Maddy were in. However, after the novelty began to die down he had returned to his previous relationship behaviour expecting Diana to be there in the background as Maddy had always been cooking, housework and not grumbling if he was out on the golf course all day.

Eventually one afternoon Diana had appeared in the Club house and confronted him angrily in front of a group of his friends. He still felt the embarrassment. Things had deteriorated after that.

He was now on his own and found himself missing, not Diana, but Maddy. She had always seemed contented with their life together. Admittedly you couldn't have called them a conventionally close couple. They both had their interests and looking back that seemed to be the really good thing about their relationship. He found himself more and more yearning back to those days, not feeling good and wondering what life would now hold for him.

The telephone rang and startled him out of his reverie. It was Grace, his daughter. Another thing he was missing was the close relationship he had had with her and her brothers until the split up between Maddy and himself.

"Hi, Grace, how are you?"

"Dad, sorry, I haven't been in touch but you know it works both ways. How are you and Diana?"

"Diana's left. I thought you knew."

Grace frowned. She did know but she had wanted him to tell her. Perhaps she was being mean but why should he get away with it.

"I had heard but you know, these days I don't believe anything until I get it directly from the parties concerned."

"Well, it's true. I feel I have made a mess of everything."

"You certainly have. Anyway, it's not worth dwelling on it. What are you doing now? Where are you living?"

"I am still in the apartment that Diana and I were sharing. She decided to go back to her daughter's house for the meantime."

"Oh, well, perhaps it's for the best."

There was a pause where both considered what to say next. Grace took the plunge.

"It's a shame, what you did caused a lot of confusion in the family. It has all been a bit upsetting."

"I feel it too. I know it's my fault. I can't tell you now how sorry I am. I hope things can improve between us. I know it will take time. Don't really know what to do."

Colin paused, he felt to continue on those lines wasn't productive. Maddy broke into his train of thought.

"Well, there is something perhaps you could help with and maybe it would improve relationships."

"Okay, tell me."

"Well, it's about Mum. She's missing."

"What do you mean missing?"

"Well, I am not sure really whether she is missing. It's just that we were in the habit of phoning each other regularly. It's now several weeks since we've spoken. No answer on her phone, nothing and it is unlike her and I can't even leave a message as the telephone connection tells me that the answering machine is full up which tells me that she is not at home and hasn't been for some time."

"Do you know any of her friends there? I thought there was an Uncle Simon that had turned up."

"I know but I never had any of his contact details or those of any of her friends."

"How was she when you spoke to her last?"

"Well, okay, though I felt there might have been something troubling her. She seemed a bit vague. When did you speak to her last?"

"Quite a while ago and it did not go well. She was still quite resentful towards me but gave me the impression she wanted to stay in France and had made some kind of life for herself. Almost proud of herself living alone out there."

"Mmmm…well, I feel I should do something. I am thinking of going out there."

"On your own?"

"Yes, Richard can't leave work and I know that Madeleine will look after Jonah for me, should he need looking after," Grace said wryly.

"Okay, I could pay your fare if you like."

"Thanks, that would help. I think I should go."

"Yes, it sounds a good idea, at least you can see if she is there but perhaps just not wanting to communicate. Unlike her I know but she did not find our break up easy."

"No." There was a long pause Grace, thinking.

"Okay, I'll go."

"Look, I'll send you some money, keep in touch. In fact, I'll buy one of the latest iPhones so you can contact me wherever you are. You know, Grace, that I love you all and I am missing your mother more than I can say. I have been stupid and realise I don't want to lose you all."

"Well, best to keep that for the moment, perhaps this will help repair things somewhat."

"Thanks, darling, I have missed you."

"Me too, Dad."

After speaking to her father Grace went to see her grandmother.

Madeleine wasn't able to help. She had had contact with her cousin Simon was when he had been in touch and told her he was going to France, back to his roots and she had not been in contact with Maddy apart from a few phone calls.

It transpired that Simon had visited Maddy. Maddy had rung and told her grandmother how pleased she was to meet him. She had also discovered that the Croft had been the home of Madeleine and Simon's grandparents, which had come as a revelation to them all. This was all news to Grace and she encouraged her grandmother to expand on her and Simon's background, realising that there was quite a large extension of her family in France. It left her wondering how many distant cousins she had.

Madeleine gave Grace Simon's home address in the Lake District and Grace drove up and visited his house. It turned out to be a wooden chalet on the side of a lake, quite remote. Nobody was there and peering in through the windows, Grace saw that it was neat and tidy as if the person living there would not be returning soon.

On her return Grace told her grandmother of her plan to go to France to see if her mother was there. If not, perhaps, Simon might be there and be able to throw some light on the matter. Hugging her, Madeleine told her to be careful.

As Grace drove off Madeleine's concern mounted together with a feeling of guilt. Since leaving France shortly before the outbreak of World War II, apart from the rare occasion speaking to Simon, she had completely lost contact with her family there. It would have consoled her somewhat to have been able to give Grace a member of her French family to contact should she need help.

-◇-

Chapter 2
Maddy

(Somewhere, No Time, No Space)

The Alignment had been a pivotal point in Earth's history, setting it on a course for its destiny. Would it be able to ascend to a harmonious natural evolution or would it descend, in other words self-destruct? So much depended on the spiritual level of its population and the population's awareness of the plight of the planet in conjunction with the decision of Earth itself.

Since the Alignment Maddy had by stages woken up to her soul reality, its history and the contract she had entered into 8500 years previously.

Having lived through many incarnations over this long period had not been easy due to the three-dimensional existences she had had to endure and the amnesia that was necessary each time she reincarnated. She found three-dimensional existence heavy and wearying. In addition, the planet was heavily steeped in continual war and at the lowest level of civilisation in her opinion.

She had to deal with memories of incarnations in different historical periods. Her perception was that not much progress had been made with regard to the human species' ability to rise above the most basic instincts. They were constantly at war in different regions all over the planet, resulting in reducing populations to primitive levels of existence.

There was also the threat of pandemics. Earth had experienced several in the last 2000 years and she knew that these were imminent due to social, scientific and technological development in the more recent history. The global population having increased to such an extent that it was now becoming difficult to feed everyone.

Reviewing her Earth experience she saw that there was a need for the global population to mature, resolve differences and work together as a species and overcome their tribal attributes and warring over land. But the fact was, she felt, they were not capable of doing so unless some major catastrophe or extraordinary event occurred which would make them have to view their lives from a completely different perspective.

The biggest handicap she perceived was the conflict with the richer nations spending on space programmes, drug development, artificial intelligence, when two-third of the world's population were starving and living at the very basic level of survival. The dichotomy was that the population was not capable of rational debate globally due to the disparity in distribution of wealth and basic education. Until mankind reached a stage when it was able to provide shelter and care for everyone equally, it would never have the opportunity to think about the deeper matters of its existence and why it was created in the first place.

The gradual realisation of her powers as a highly ascended ancient enabled her to assimilate her memories without experiencing the overload that would have occurred to her physical brain in the lower dimensions. Some of her incarnations were fascinating, others terrifying as in the Cathar period and more recently the wars over religion during the sixteenth century. One incarnation in particular though amused her, linking her present incarnation with that of an earlier one, 3000 years ago in Egypt.

Archaeologists (twenty-first century) had recently unearthed her own sarcophagus in which her physical body had been laid to allow her soul to return to source. The archaeologists identified their find as a female mummy 3000 years old. The report stated that the female was a singer, one of several hundred, that took it in turns to sing in the temple every day to pacify the gods with a sweet voice. They were an elite group of women who were encouraged to dress in a slightly provocative way to assure the approval of the god which included satisfying his sexual appetite.[1]

Maddy remembered the actual facts.

Yes, she had been a singer in the temple, though she had not referred to it as a temple. It was actually a laboratory producing sound wave frequencies.

The singers were trained in ascendency, their singing producing the specific frequency to keep the energy of the planet stable and its population healthy. She thought in retrospect that it was like placating the gods but the fact was it was a scientific programme.

There were singers placed round the planet in the many pyramids of that time, all keeping, via resonance, the energy the planet and universe gave to all life forms. The resonance acted on the DNA in all things giving Earth an equanimity of existence as it was then but was not now in the twenty-first century.

Maddy remembered her life at that time and how hard it had been apart from the singing. She was an adept and had been sent by the ancients with her father at that time. He was a priest who had been reincarnated to give a depth to the chanting to raise the resonance of the pyramid laboratory. Life on Earth for her had led to her dying eventually of blocked arteries due to the diet she had had to endure, one fact the archaeologists who made the discovery verified.

The artifacts the archaeologist found on her skeleton they had interpreted as jewellery due to her high status. However, this was untrue. The artifacts were actually identity objects of the escorts that accompanied her on her journey to Earth when she had been summoned there. After her death, as a mark of respect, they had put some of these on her when they placed her in the sarcophagus.

Emerging from her perusal of these memories and her present incarnation she had begun to recognise her capabilities. Her powers were exceptional and exceeded those of Malachi/Michael her Marechal guardian from the original initiation of her contract. She was able to step up to the highest levels, travel backward and forward through time, interdimensionally, and was able to use the crossing point of light which was a different way of travelling from that which had brought her to Earth in the Egyptian period. At that time (being outside of space time constrictions) she had come via Nibiru having been ordered to consult with the ancients on a matter concerning the Nibiruns who were exploiting Earth resources, taking gold and tampering with the genetics of the indigenous species on Earth. She could see now that it was elements of the Nibirun DNA that had created the warlike aggressive traits that lingered in the current world population and hampered its ascendancy.

Nibiru was a troublesome planet, it had a 3600 Earth year orbit around the sun, the centre of the solar system that included Earth. It had its problems in the ozone layer of its planet, which had eroded and therefore was not protecting them when at the extreme points of its orbit, when it was closest to the sun and then farther away. The gold they needed, which Earth had in abundance, they converted to monoatomic gold, a white powder which had unusual qualities, which they shot into their atmosphere and which sealed their ozone layer, thereby healing it. However they were doing this without considering the consequences it had for Earth.[2]

Other extra-terrestrials had also tampered with Earth, one consequence of which was in her latest incarnation when she had had to be removed to a different dimension. Maddy remembered the reasons, the crippling gynaecological problems that had manifested in her body from the age of 11 through to 34. The guardians in consultation transported her to another dimension and put her in the hands of a reincarnated ancient specialist. He saved her life and that of the foetus she lost in an ectopic pregnancy, Magda, who grew up in that other dimension. She remembered her dreams of the white world, the place Magda had been taken to from that dimension and the visits she had made to her daughter in dreams.

In that life, in that dimension, Maddy had lurched from one medical catastrophe to another but each time the ancients had sent her a specialist to save her life. These were, she was now remembering, always the same ancient guardian whom she knew in this incarnation as Ralph.

She knew this splitting off into another dimension had had to happen in order to keep the present incarnation on track for the Alignment.

Comparing the two dimensions, reviewing her present dimensional incarnation and the medical problems she had experienced, she realised Ralph had appeared to help her. She then saw her life settle with some stability and asked the ancients for peace to live out the rest of that dimensional life.

Taking a sweeping view of all of her dimensional existences she saw them come into being and fade and the strongest endure, one of which was the incarnation she was experiencing now.

Having regained her memory she was troubled about the state of the planet Earth and its ascendency. Something was holding it back and it was not just the lack of high vibration. There seemed to be a complete denial in the consciousness of the population about the state of the Earth. However, climate change was beginning to affect the planet more and more, disasters occurring at closer intervals, creating a huge demand on government disaster relief funds.

Her thoughts raised memories of when Earth was created and the joy of the ancients in this beautiful blue planet and its potential to provide a base for evolutionary experiment to provide a library store for the DNA of all species. It should have been a place for refuge and rejuvenation of pure consciousness. Its beauty and possibilities, though viewed favourably by the majority of the universal population, had been observed by other acquisitive universes and dimensions from its very inception. This had allowed it to become a target for pillaging many times.

Waking from her reverie she realised she needed to see the ancient guardians, in particular Overseer Fraterne Nammu and her guardian Marechal Malachi and view the developments on Earth after the Alignment. Looking into the lives of her Earth family from where she was, she saw how troubled her daughter Grace was and knew that soon she would have to meet her and explain as best she could.

Currently Nammu and Malachi were on a satellite orbiting Venus which the ancients had established as a temporary base for overseeing the current situation on Earth. Their other meetings had been in the Reunion Chamber, a place outside of space/time linear existence. Her understanding was that Magda was on the satellite too so she could combine the two visits.

Emerging from the *Mists of Memory* Maddy set in the coordinates to step down to the lower level.

-◇-

Chapter 3
Maddy Meets Magda

(Venus – place other dimension (POD))

Maddy entered the room. The girl was sitting by a window, though Maddy thought it was more like a port hole on a ship. There was a view through it onto a planet which they appeared to be orbiting. The planet looked red hot and molten, spurting intermittently what were probably clouds of noxious gases.

Turning to the girl, instinctively Maddy knew this was her daughter Magda and she had been to visit her before, in fact many times in lucid dreams during this incarnation. However, she knew that this was not the place where she had visited her and it must be some kind of holding station they had both been brought to.

The girl was serene, wearing a gown that glistened. She was so beautiful, ethereal, like a fairy, pale with gold sparkling hair held back by a circlet of tiny pearls. She glided towards Maddy and clasped her arms around her waist and rested her head on Maddy's shoulder.

"Mother."

As she held the girl in her arms, an overwhelming feeling of completion encompassed Maddy. She gazed intently at Magda.

"I am your daughter, Magda, Mother, don't you remember?"

"In this incarnation I am feeling very strange, I do remember but at the same time I don't. I have memories, dreams of travelling somewhere."

Maddy let her eyes roam around the room, taking in the whiteness of everything and looking through the window. Holding on to Magda she watched as the clouds of gas rose and fell like mountainous waves of water, blistering in an unreal light.

"…but nothing seems solid."

"We are really here together."

"Tell me what your life is like? You say I am your mother, tell me first what you understand by that."

"You have always been with me from when I was tiny. You came to see me on the planet that is my home in the creche – there is a nursery creche there where all the babies are cared for – so I know that when I say you have always been with me, you first came to me there."

"In the nursery creche?"

"Yes."

"And then?"

"Well, little ones are moved to small rooms, usually four or five in each room and from there they share lessons and play and eat together in small groups."

"And I continued to visit you?"

"Yes, frequently, all of us had visits from our mothers. The visits continued through my life until now, along with study and duties. The group considers itself a family."

Maddy interrupted.

"What are you studying?"

"We all study Universal Law and Physics."

"I see." Maddy recalled from her soul's existence undergoing the same training but she asked Magda.

"Exactly what does that mean?"

"We are beings that co-exist and think as one. It is complex obviously, we have to learn about the physiological and biological structure of the universe and the language that we share. Basically it is all held in our DNA – like electrical antennae. I have no understanding of the Earth, Ki-Gi-Kia, that you have incarnated to over millennia other than what has been revealed to me in my education."

Maddy was beginning to feel very weary, glancing around her attention waning. She was still feeling the effects post Alignment coming into her soul existence. Maddy's memory was tingling, feeling a peculiar, dreamlike, other reality. All she had recollected with Simon and Malachi came flooding into her consciousness and was integrating. She felt synapses in her head alive and snapping across junction points.

"Why is everything white?"

"Actually it's not – the vibration is high so it gives everything that appearance. You are on the seventh dimension level. Everything is not dense as it is on the lower third dimension you have become used to in your present and past incarnations. Nothing you see is solid here, actually even in the third dimension nothing is solid in the way you think you perceive it. It is just a mass of particles vibrating at a very specific frequency."

"So where am I?"

"You are on a holding POD, that is 'Place/Other Dimension' orbiting Venus, the fourth planet from the sun in this solar system. We are orbiting Venus in a specific stratosphere which has similar qualities to that on earth so we can sustain some presence for you here. We are here because the planet you have been living on in this incarnation is going through a transfiguration. Earth is in a state of 'in-determination'. It is ascending and descending in the moment. Where its potential eventually lies is not fixed yet. You know that, they have called it the 'Alignment'. You were part of a plan to save the planet from descending but whether you were able to is still in the balance."

"Yes, I remember now. You refer to 'they'."

"You are one of 'they', tell me you have already become aware of your eternal existence, your soul."

"Yes, but it remains inchoate to me at the moment. I can't grasp the whole story, as it were, the reason."

"Let it be, it will come back fully."

"Am I supposed to stay here in this place?"

"Well, it is up to you and the ancients, you will need to make up your mind."

"I am concerned about my Earth daughter…"

Here Maddy looked at the girl sensing a strange feeling and hoping she had not upset her.

"I am sorry I don't mean to upset you but I have a terrestrial daughter and two sons. They will be worrying about me. How do I reassure them?"

"It's difficult. You have a choice – you can return and live out your life with your family there or stay here and consider some potential alternatives or return to the ancient domain."

"What would it mean to my family on Earth if I don't return?"

"You will become an unexplained mystery, disappear, that's all."

"That's all!"

Maddy was thinking about the stress it would cause, especially to her daughter Grace.

"But it could cause huge consternation and heartache."

"Have you thought that that might be part of their lives' plan? You know we all have contracts for our lives and lessons within them. This may be a lesson for them that they have to overcome."

"It seems a pretty brutal one."

"There are far more brutal lessons."

Magda raised her eyebrows and searched deep within Maddy's eyes. Maddy felt Magda's eyes piercing into her and realised reluctantly what Magda was getting at.

"Well, you could stay here and observe the destiny of the planet and your family and what happens to them."

"Yes, I am realising the skills I have."

"Oh, yes, you can travel through time and inter dimensionally. You just have to return to us fully. Your daughter on Earth has your DNA and therefore carries many traits that will enable you to connect with her."

Looking at Maddy, whose face by now was pale and taut with stress, Magda continued,

"I think enough for the time being. Go and rest, we call it re-energising and then I will take you to meet the Overseers. You will recognise them or let's say your soul will, so don't be apprehensive. They are your equals, your soul group."

-◇-

Maddy felt strange, strange in that she did not feel tired in the way she normally would have done but fatigued, mind weary. Magda led her to another room and she lay down on a ledge that protruded from the wall. To her the rooms felt very cell like, with no furnishings, however, the mattress and cover on the ledge were soft and comforting and she soon became drowsy. She fell into a dreamlike trance with images passing through her mind. As she fell into a deeper sleep it came to her that perhaps she was dying and yet...

Dreaming...I am falling in space, the Earth appearing as it was meant to have evolved, a paradise for the beings of the universe to visit and re-energise; its population balanced and grown in symbiosis with the environment, the Earth as it should be, verdant and exotic in its flora and fauna, the people beautiful and healthy, their needs catered for by their interaction, gentle and loving to everything that exists.

Then the view changes, seeing it now, vastly over populated in proportion to the environment, air and oceans polluted and plundered of their natural resources – recovery from which hung like a dead weight on the verge of dropping into oblivion.

The contrast was heart breaking and I came to weeping.

...and was weeping still when Magda came to fetch her to take her to the Overseers.

"How would it be if they hadn't polluted this planet?" asked Maddy.

Magda having an insight to Maddy's dream was expecting her question.

"Its natural evolution would have ensured a healthy population with resources to match that population. When it reached a maximum, if that happened, then the Overseers would have consulted the population and with its consent moved a percentage to another planet that had been prepared for them."

"And the people would have agreed to that?"

"They would have been prepared. Management of planet population is one of the priorities of the Ancients along with natural evolution of the species.

Unfortunately, on Earth, it is not only the planet's natural evolution that is of concern. Due to the genetic engineering carried out by previous visitors to the planet, some unhealthy psychological features and aggressive traits developed in the indigenous species. The people on it have been constantly at war for thousands of years and recently developed nuclear power. That has set alarm bells off throughout the universe as the people of Earth now have the ability to destroy their own planet and if that happened it would set off ripples disrupting their universe and beyond. To make matters worse, the planet is now over populated and the situation is becoming critical."

"So what you are saying is that the people on Earth are about to destroy their species but why has it become over populated if you say that natural evolution would have taken care of that and the Overseers would have dealt with it?"

"Well, as you are aware the Halqu, the most recent hostile visiting extra-terrestrials, cast a net around Earth so that they had control at the time of the Alignment. Luckily, we, with your help destroyed the net and allowed the planet to regain its natural evolutionary state. It was only at the time of Alignment that we were able to step in and help.

The Alignment, should there be no further interference, will allow the Earth to ascend and will prevent those things which are cyclic happening again. There have been many civilisations on Earth that go back millions of years and each civilisation has wiped itself out and the Earth has had to start all over again. This time, however, we are hoping that it will be left in peace and the effect of that will ripple out into the Universe, this Harmonic Universe, which will ascend along with Earth.

Invasion of the planet by extra-terrestrials and stories about the end of days are presented to your Earth population through the visual fictitious media. People do not think deeper but this fiction is based on this history. It is the way the Halqu have desensitised the population to control it by fear.

We see all, are all, and you will too once you are fully awakened."

Magda paused and received a summons to take Maddy to the upper chamber.

-◇-

Chapter 4
Maddy Visits Nammu

Magda led Maddy to a platform and Maddy felt herself lifted in space. She felt she was not going up or down, it did not seem that the platform had moved at all, in fact perhaps it did not have to. They entered a large space which was empty and had no windows. It was lit softly by some source which she could not discern.

For a moment something alerted her. She turned and the air shimmered and an image materialised. A tall lean man approached her. He was very handsome. He had greying neatly cut hair and was clean shaven, wearing a beautifully cut business suit, white shirt and blue silk tie with matching handkerchief in his suit breast pocket. His shoes were highly polished black lace ups. His right hand extended towards her and he took her hand in his and placed his other hand over hers. Maddy was overcome, his presence was making her whole body tingle with anticipation and the thought jumped into her head – of what! Having incarnated so many times into the human species she realised it was the libido in her three dimensional Earth frame that was responding.

Malachi observed the greeting and looked towards Isolde and rolled his eyes. How clever he thought of Nammu to overwhelm Maddy completely by emanating an abundance of erotic reassurance.

Isolde, like Malachi, was a Marechal, a further guardian to watch over Maddy. She was sitting on a ledge in the form of her favourite persona, a ragamuffin looking black cat with a wizarding lightening streak of ginger down her forehead. Malachi had decided to stay in the human form Maddy was most familiar with, that of Michael.

Ethereally, both were hovering out of sight observing the exchange between Maddy and Nammu.

Nammu was murmuring soft words of encouragement to Maddy.

"You are still seeing and feeling with your three-dimensional human form. You must get back to where you were."

"I am getting there but it is taking a toll on my frequency levels. What has been happening since the Alignment? There are a few other things I need to understand to help me move on a little more quickly."

Nammu continued, "In this Harmonic Universe in your present, incarnation circumstances became complicated. The Halqu caught up with you and were trying to capture your DNA to experiment with. They were unable to use you but unfortunately left your reproductive organs in a bad state. However, you became pregnant with Magda and there were difficulties and we had to remove you to another dimension. Your role in the Alignment was of paramount importance and we needed your full concentration on that when the time came."

"I understand that – what you are saying is obvious. I am becoming more aware of my true self, my soul state and ancestry. But what about my daughters in the different dimensions?"

"They have their own destinies, you have to work on detachment. Your incarnations have been numerous and intense and each had multiple future potentials which have been playing out in concurrent dimensions. As an ancient when you have regained total recall you will be able to harmonise your perceptions. But now you must trust in the process."

"But we would also like to give you some examples of the plight of earth and that requires inter-dimensional travel and transfiguration. You might not have regained that just yet."

"I am assuming that I can do that?"

"Yes, every human has the potential to access it. In your incarnations you have not studied the mechanics of Universal Physics. The scientists in the present time period are just getting to grips with this advanced physics. But you did study it, just as Magda has in soul state."

"Well, refresh me so that I can understand more quickly."

"It is a question of understanding light and how it travels rather than thinking about speed. Whether we time travel or pass inter dimensionally, we start the travel in the conventional way from your Earth perspective, that is, let's call it a vehicle though, we are actually standing in a special kind of space. Some of you Earth people know about this space, those sensitives amongst you. They call it a Merkaba."[3]

"We approach the speed of light but to travel at the speed of light our bodies would disintegrate. We have to change molecularly in order to continue to withstand this, otherwise we would not be able to cover the distances space and dimensional travel require. We are not really talking about travel here at all we are talking about 're-placement in space'."

"As I said we approach the speed of light, we set our destination and then convert. Most simply put, at that moment 'pure thought' takes over and the distance is covered by thought. Approaching the destination we convert back and speed is reduced conventionally. Obviously it has an effect on the cellular body. That is why to travel time or dimensionally, the traveller must have developed the body's resonance, the energy level or frequency to withstand it."

"You know all of this as you are an Ancient, you will remember. As you have been living many three-dimensional incarnations, your cellular body has adapted but it will revert to wherever you wish to be. Three dimensional frequency restricts the ability of consciousness to see reality – memory is lost of your soul life. To remember all incarnations requires ascending to very high frequencies close to source."

"To do what you did at the Alignment we had to recall you to your ancient vibration, that is why we sent a light worker and Malachi to work with you and raise your level. Anyway, you will remember, it will soon be recalled to you as an ancient."

Maddy was caught in her thoughts but said, "What now?"

"Well, you have many options; return to the ancient domain, continue in one dimension or move between dimensions in this sector. What do you want to do? You must listen to your soul speaking to you. Eventually you will do what is right for you."

"I want to see Grace and my family to reassure them. I will have to tell them what has happened and introduce them to all of these concepts. I can foresee that they most probably will find it very difficult. I think at the moment they may be alarmed at my disappearance. I must have been gone for some time now?"

"Yes, nearly an Earth year and you are right, they are now looking for you. In fact Grace has arrived in France and is meeting Malachi and Simon now."

Maddy caught Nammu looking to the side of the room and at the same time caught a glimpse of Malachi/Michael standing beside a large cat. Puzzled she blinked twice thinking she was seeing things and glanced back to Nammu.

"I understand your desire to go back and should you need help with your family consult Malachi and we will work something out. So be it, we will meet soon anyway."

Nammu raised his arm saying, "All time, all things are now and complete." He then dissolved into the atmosphere.

Maddy watched him disappear and turned to Magda who was looking at her with some amusement, noting Maddy's struggle from incarnation to soul.

"You will soon re-accustom yourself to our ways, now your ways again," she added, sagely.

"Come, we will return to my rooms and set the course for your return to Earth and your family."

-◇-

Chapter 5
Nammu Reviews

(Venus POD)

Nammu was standing at the vast viewing window on the holding station looking down on Venus. The opaque sulphuric acid clouds were swirling beneath his feet, from time to time gaps appearing in them, revealing the red hot surface of the planet.

He was contemplating the visit he had just had with Maddy, Magda, Malachi and Isolde.

"Well, what do you think?" he said as he turned towards Malachi.

"At this moment I think Maddy is wrestling with her concerns for her daughters Magda and Grace and in particular how she is going to tell Grace in her present incarnation about who she is and her soul history. Grace is unaware of all of this and Maddy needs to deal with the situation. Magda is in a different dimension from Grace. I assume Magda is capable of coming down to Level 3? So there is the potential perhaps of her meeting Grace should Maddy consider it necessary."

Malachi turned to Nammu looking for a response.

"Yes, Magda is able to do that. I think, however, that we need to have a plan for the way forward. First, Maddy has to decide which potential probability to choose. Then we can sort out Grace and Magda. I know Magda will do anything to support Maddy but Grace coming from her timeline may be unpredictable. Leaving all that for now let's review the situation on Earth, how it is faring after the Alignment."

Malachi followed Nammu to a large screen to the side of the chamber. The screen became active at their approach and showed holographic scenes currently occurring on Earth. It showed a global view of the planet highlighting areas of warfare and civil unrest; climate, volcanic and plate disruption, social inequality, areas of poverty compared with affluent areas of excess. It pinpointed regions where huge earth excavation projects were taking place – Nammu turned to Malachi.

"It is disturbing how bad things are. The planet is now over populated for its size despite all the deaths due to war and terrorist activities and unavailability of good health care globally."

"One of the worrying developments is that the planet now has access to what they call the internet. This has surpassed and supplanted all other types of communication and is cross cultural and cross means."

"What do you mean?" queried Nammu.

"Everybody is obsessed by the media through television, mobile phones and game devices. Mainly war games. They are becoming totally disconnected from the planet and their biological roots. Technology has overtaken them and is splitting their allegiances; broadcasting war, terrorism and crime constantly in news bulletins has begun to desensitise the population. They are all frightened about everyday life, expecting some calamity to confront them. They are not living their lives fully.

What does that do to the evolution of their bodies if they are not using them as they were meant to? They have devices pinned to their ears or special viewing glasses or implants…if the body is not used and it was made to be used, how will it evolve, survive?"

Nammu answered, "There will be a move to concentrate the population into mega cities in the interests of safety. This will mean that those in power can control the population which could be one of the ultimate aims of the Halqu. The planet will become entirely technology based, then everything controlled by computers, literally everything, farming, food production and communication."

"Which brings us back to the reason that the Halqu wanted access to the portals and gates at the Alignment. My point is that the body of the homo sapiens is a working instrument specifically designed to evolve in symbiosis with the planet Earth. Because the population has some of the 'Annunaki DNA' at a certain point of development they will have to deal with that dilemma of decisions. Enki wrote his book and tried to warn future civilisations not to blow themselves to pieces as his species destroyed Earth before."[4]

'The Halqu, a rebellious cult of the Annunaki, developed genetically and technologically and lost the symbiosis they should have had with their own planet."

Nammu paused…

"It seems we are playing a waiting game. We will have to give it a year Earth time and then review again." He turned away from the screen.

Malachi followed him.

"Is there anything we can do in the meantime apart from assisting Maddy to wake up further and attend to her decision?"

"If the planet manages to ascend then we are relieved of any action. Our main concern is if the planet descends. There remains a certain percentage of the population who are sufficiently spiritually ascended but not quite there yet to go to levels four or five dimensionally but they need help and teaching. They don't deserve to die as they are trying to reach that level."

"Then could we make the plans for moving them here?"

"No, they need to be on a planet that resembles Earth environmentally so their experiences are relevant to what they are used to. Also, we will need teachers to guide them and help them towards ascension. We need to find one of our growing planets to which we can take them to and a team of Marechal to guide them."

"Do we have them, these growing planets?"

"Yes, several within this sector, haven't you been aware of them? The Pleiades has one of its suns, Alcyone, which has Eta Tauri which might be appropriate and Vega in the Lyra constellation may have a family of planets and asteroid belt similar to Earth's sun. One of those might be suitable. And we mustn't forget, Isolde comes from there, Avyon, the planet of cats. She might be prepared to go with the team as a watcher. Cats are special guards that deal with violence."[5]

"I see the Shuruppak are looking after themselves, building bunkers. They think that is going to save them? The Halqu maybe having some influence on them, probably giving them misleading information. The Shuruppak are still blind to their devices. We need to keep an eye on them. They may have some kind of portal they can access or even be trying to get the Shuruppak, their contact on Earth to activate one. Don't forget it would still be to their advantage if they could."[6]

"Well, what do you think?"

"Not much change at the moment. It may be too soon?" asked Malachi.

"We need to keep an eye on the bunker builders, the Shuruppak," Nammu said ironically. "They might be able to show us if the Halqu are still here. They are the rich who can afford a place in them. Not only are they building bunkers but also star-ships to escape from the planet, eco systems in space by which they can travel until they find a suitable planet to resettle on to rule! Good luck to them if they take that route as many generations will pass and who knows how the species will evolve trapped in such a restricted environment.

"The best way would be to take people off through the stargates and portals but that requires them ascending to much higher frequencies as we discussed. They are presently unaware because the Halqu have purposely kept them uninformed."

Malachi asked, "Then what should we do, can we do?"

"Well, nothing at this precise moment other than observe as we may not need to do anything."

"Yes, but mightn't it be a good idea to take some of the more enlightened as early as possible so that they can form a reception for the others if the worst happens?"

"Mmmmm...you have a point."

Nammu paced, unsettled, then decided, "We will send a scouting team to find a suitable planet. You must speak to Maddy and see if she would be prepared eventually to go to the new planet and start setting up the new settlement there. It could be a choice for her. Think about her daughter and family, it may be we can use them…"

"What's your thinking there?" Malachi asked.

"Perhaps Maddy and a team could find those of the population sufficiently spiritually awakened. They can present ideas of what might happen and what they can do to combat it, realising their true selves. As such it is a work in progress as to whether the population can be reconnected to their biological awareness."

"We will also send star seeds into their next generation – they will have the component part in their DNA which will influence their thinking, it will change it and make access to the spiritual dimension easier. Remember, technology has its place but not when it takes over."

"Yes, I see," Malachi responded. "I must go and see how Maddy is getting on with her return to the village and meeting her daughter and husband. I will try and find out if she has had any further thoughts about her choice."

"Yes, let me know and then we must give her some insight into her previous lives so that she can further trigger her source body. We must also fill her in regarding the betrayal lineage which I can foresee is looming in her near future. If you remember you helped her escape from the massacre in France on St. Bartholomew's Eve."

"Yes, I remember, very confusing for her at the time and dangerous, we got her out just in time."

Malachi was just about to depart when an alarm activated; both moved to the console to see where it was coming from. The signal was coming from the area at the juncture of the North Atlantic and Arctic Oceans where the main island of Iceland was located.

The invocation accompanying it was received from an insider in the Shuruppak, who owned and managed most of the large global corporations and who heavily influenced government and banking decisions.

"What is going on?"

Looking at the coded message Nammu related.

"It looks like there is increased activity on the Ark Project. Remember, this project was set up in the early seeding of the planet to collect the DNA of species as they evolved. It exists in the North Atlantic. It looks like it is warning of an imminent extinction event; so who or what has made them aware of it?"

"Who would benefit from it?" asked Malachi.

"Could the Halqu want to take over the planet and populate it with the genetic hybrids they are experimenting with? Perhaps they have achieved this. Reducing the population or annihilating it could mean they are planning to repopulate the planet with their own species; have they realised that they can't get back to their own planet?"

"We are of little consequence to visitors now as we have not enough resources for them to convert other than perhaps harvesting us for food. Macabre thought but there are infinite species in the universe whose eating requirements are inconceivable. Precession has occurred and Earth is now under the constellation of Aquarius. So far, apart from some pretty bizarre weather events across the planet, it seems to be passing through this period without undue disaster, though there has been some significant loss of lives already due to natural disasters."

"They are of course still in the 2000 year phase of increased frequency level which accounts for the increase in mental health problems which has given rise to suicidal tendencies in a considerable percentage of the population."

"Although there has been a great deal of scaremongering information on their social network about Niburu crashing into the planet, it is nowhere near enough for anybody to be worried about. Anyway, it won't be crashing into Earth but passing it by. It will of course cause a lot of disturbances but by the time that point is reached the population should have the technology or have ascended sufficiently to deal with any destruction. Anyway we are talking about some considerable time yet."

"No, there is something else going on and..." Nammu paused thoughtfully. "...and what we said previously, I have a sense that it is to do with our old friends, the Halqu, it may be that their own planet is now beyond recovery."

"But I thought we had dealt with them at the Alignment."

"Yes, but you are forgetting they are amazingly cunning. It is they who have placed holographic illusions on the population from time to time for their own devices. They still want the planet, I think to start afresh. Once they have sent their minions, the *Shuruppak* on their way on the star ships to return them as their slaves once they have taken over the planet, they may destroy the remaining population and restart the civilisation as a replica of their home planet."

"We must find out what the situation is on their home planet."

Nammu set a string of co-ordinates into the console.

-◇-

Chapter 6
Return of the Halqu

The Halqu thwarted in their attempt to control Earth's portals at the time of the Alignment, retreated to their outpost within their home planet's star system. This was a similar situation to the holding station orbiting Venus (POD) occupied by the Ancestors, Nammu and company. However, the planet of the Halqu had deteriorated dramatically and was on the verge of disintegration.

The Council of the Halqu had been summoned as had Lord Andrews, their Earth contact under their control. Lord Raymond Andrews was the leader of the Sharappuk, the small percentage of the population on Earth who were very wealthy and in control by subterfuge of all the major corporations and governments of the world.

Lord Andrews and Maddy were descended from the Ramoindine Dynasty by different genealogical routes though unaware of each other's existence in this incarnation.

The Ramoindine Dynasty was descended from ancestors of the original guardians of their lineage, the Cloister of Lilith, which was formed to guard the Seal, Lilith and her soul and its incarnations through to the twenty-first century when she was activated to protect the Alignment and the ascension of

Earth to a higher dimension. Allegiances were split soon after the formation of the Cloister when one of the original guardians (Lord Andrews' ancestor) betrayed the secrets of the Cloister of Lilith to the extra-terrestrial visitors, the Halqu.

The original betrayer was persuaded by the promise of the secret of eternal life. In a previous colonisation of the planet, visitors genetically engineered the DNA of the indigenous population and created the Earthlings as they were known to them. However, the Earthlings were denied the component in their DNA to have eternal life, 'to eat of the tree of life'. Seduced by this promise Lord Andrew's ancestors ensured the Halqu of a supply of information about Maddy down through her incarnations.

Vaxchtajn was the leader of the Halqu. A fearsome entity in appearance and energetic force. His breathing rasped and his speech was staccato and clicking in expression. Adjusting their communication devices Vaxchtajn bellowed.

"So what happened!?" referring to the Alignment.

"I thought you had tracked the earthling female, the Seal."

Lord Andrews stepped towards Vaxchtajn.

"They moved very quickly, we didn't know exactly who the Seal was until the day."

"How could you have missed her?"

"Our French agent had only met her once and somehow had no way of getting close to verify his suspicions. Nammu and the ancestors had Marechal throwing them off track."

"It is unacceptable!"

Lord Andrews was now becoming seriously agitated. He had seen others disappear in front of him by a blink of Vaxchtajn's eye. He was glancing around for an escape route, thinking his fate was now at hand. Vaxchtajn's bodyguards were moving closer.

Vaxchtajn held out a tentacle hand, the bodyguards stopped moving forward.

"Sources tell me that the ancestors had assembled a protective measure around the planet to ensure its ascension. Why did we not know about this?"

This was news to Lord Andrews. Obviously Vaxchtajn had agents on Earth other than himself; he began to feel even more dispensable. Speaking up, he replied, "It will still be a difficult time on Earth. There are many changes occurring in the planet's evolutionary time line along with potential ascension. Climate changes due to precession and pollution are taking their toll. The Ancestors anticipate its survival along with a healthy proportion of the 'Earthlings'. They expect them eventually to continue their natural evolution in symbiosis with the planet despite the visitor's genetic engineering on them."

Vaxchtajn rose, expanding to his full height and width. Lord Andrews looking up at him judged him to be more than 8 ft with limbs flailing, spindly and barbed. His head was large and bald and his skin grey. His face was dominated by huge ice blue eyes with double eyelids. Like a reptile thought Lord Andrews.

Vaxchtajn shouted, "We must take Earth! We need to repopulate our species there. It is the only planet that has an atmosphere closest to our needs. We can adjust the chemical components of its atmosphere to those sustainable to us once we possess it."

"Our planet has died as has our race that remained there. Those that survived are living on holding stations and ships in deep space waiting for our summons. They need to be re-established. We can modulate earth," he reiterated. Turning to Lord Andrews he continued.

"You must re-congregate the Sharappuk. Tell them what we are doing and re-energise them with promises of status in the future community on Earth. Do you understand? We will engineer things on Earth which will mean that the surface of the planet will be cleansed, rid of its current species. We will take the Sharrapuk off the planet before this happens and then return them afterwards to work for us. Do you understand?"

Vaxchtajn repeated with emphasis.

"Yes, my Lord."

"Leave. We will contact you again soon and we can consolidate our plans. Go," he commanded.

Lord Andrews bowed, turned and went to the transfiguration booth to return to Earth. He was nervous. He knew their plans to ship the Sharappuk off the planet and to let Earth experience an extinction event. It would be contrived by the Halqu to coincide with the planet's natural evolutionary events thus not warn the population of the Halqu's plans. It would destroy all life on earth.

He had been instructed to coordinate the Arks containing the DNA of every living thing on Earth. These were now complete and he saw the Halqu plans clearly, their repopulation of the planet after the extinction event. In space/time he also saw how quickly this would be achieved by them with the technology they had at their disposal, being able to move in time and dimensions. Thousands of years of recovery could happen on Earth but to them it would be but a moment.

Lord Andrews knew that the time was now approaching fast and he had much to do.

-◇-

Chapter 7
Philippa

Hertfordshire, England, 2013.

Back in the study of his country house Lord Andrews sat in his favourite chair. Momentarily he felt safe and protected by the room which he had created as his escape from the world and his family. He closed his eyes soaking up the ambience, wondering how he would feel if he had to give all this up. This was on the cards now after his interview with Vaxchtajn. His feelings were surprising to him, emotional and erratic, wondering why he had pursued this course.

He could recall all of his incarnations and he remembered, that on a whim, at the very beginning he had betrayed the Cloister when they chose Lilith as the Seal, now incarnated as Maddy.

Philippa, his only daughter, was a fiery spirit and could originally like Maddy have been one of the chosen Seals. At that time he had been surprised at the depth of his anger. Now he realised that things would never be the same.

Niggling him was what to do about Philippa now. His wife had left him long ago. He was feeling lonely at that moment and missed Philippa despite the troublesome behaviour she had exhibited increasingly over the recent years as she had become a teenager. He knew all teenagers could be difficult but her behaviour probably had more to do with an experience when she was a toddler.

He knew, though she had never raised the subject, that she had caught him with the visitors, members of the Halqu, when she was a tiny child. The country house was a vast mansion and staircases led off the entrance hall to a landing above. It was only when she started to have nightmares that were so bad that she had been referred to a child psychologist that he realised that one night she had crept out onto the landing and saw him talking to the Halqu below.

The child psychologist had told his wife that Philippa's nightmares consisted of visions of huge monsters flailing about and chasing her. He could hardly tell her that they weren't nightmares but reality. The Halqu do appear as huge monsters and he knew that with their sixth sense they would have known she was watching and to keep their cover they had imprinted that image into her memory and would make her appear delusional to those she confided to.

This of course had deeply disturbed him but under their control he knew the limits of their empathy and lack of patience. His life was constantly under threat and he was helpless to do anything about it. He felt deep sorrow and grief about what he had done to Philippa.

What to do? He asked himself.

If he told her the truth of her heritage, her soul story and the ancient history tracked back to the formation of the Cloister and the contract concerning the Alignment, what would her reaction be?

At the moment Philippa was quite happily enrolled in a private school in Hertfordshire and for all appearances seemed to be doing well on all levels. Though he and his wife were estranged they did still communicate about her. His wife, who was fully aware of the Halqu and his relationship with them, saw her on a regular basis and had reported only recently that all was well.

Pressing, however, were the demands of Vaxchtajn, so deciding to shelve his thoughts about Philippa for the moment, he thought he must press on with the instructions from Vaxchtajn. Anyway, if it came to it at the last minute he would have to kidnap Philippa and take her with him to wherever the Halqu decided he was to go.

Turning to his computer he sent out a coded message to all members of the Sharappuk relating Vaxchtajn's instructions and telling them to get ready to leave for the various meeting points that they had been allotted.

-◇-

Philippa Andrews had been sent to boarding school when she was eight years old. At the time the reasons for her going away were a bit vague to her, other than that her mother had decided to leave the family home in Bedfordshire. Initially she had gone with her mother to live in London but her parents decided eventually that they wanted her to be in a settled environment and not caught up in their relationship difficulties.

So, here she was. Now at the age of 17 in her final year at school. She had spent her holidays alternately with her mother and father. Recently, however, she had found the time spent with either parent disturbing and she had become troublesome to them on purpose to test them. She did not really understand why she found them difficult to be with more so with her father than her mother.

When she went to stay with her father at the country estate, she found herself subjected to the violent nightmares she had experienced when she was much younger. These had dissipated since she had been at boarding school.

The routine of life at the school was full and she was always busy, healthily tired and slept well. Her prowess at sports assisted with her well-being. She did not like spending time in the country. Although she was able to go riding frequently and go walking on the estate the mystery was that she found being there psychologically disturbing.

Her father was quite distant though he did make an effort to eat with her on a daily basis but she found herself in the company of the staff more than of him. She passed a great deal of time in the kitchen with Amy the cook/housekeeper who had made it the cosiest place in the house.

Philippa liked her school. It was set on an old country estate in Hertfordshire. She had made friends with several girls and the teachers were very pleasant, especially as she excelled at academic studies, music and on the sports field. She was very good at hockey and tennis and played the piano. Currently she was applying for entry to one of the major universities.

Recently she and her friends were allowed to venture out of the school on weekends and were able to go into the local town to shop and pass time in the coffee shops.

The school also had inter school championships with neighbouring secondary schools and she and her friends had made other friends out of school. On Saturdays they often met their new friends in town.

Philippa's father was an astro-physicist and by natural inclination, probably, inherited from him she had excelled at science and was particularly interested in astronomy. One of her recent school projects was about climate change and the possibility that the movement of the constellations had caused this. She had studied ancient civilisations that were obsessed with observation of the stars.

One of the friends she had made from the other schools she played against was Jonah Williams and they met from time to time on the Saturday outings into town. He attended a state grammar school in a neighbouring town. Their friendship had grown out of a mutual interest in the subject. He had told her of an association he belonged to that met regularly to go star gazing. There were trips at night and he had told her of one coming soon and she was trying to get permission to go to it. One of her teachers, keen on encouraging her interest, was planning to accompany her so it made getting permission from her parents easier.

Jonah, her friend, was looking forward to it as well. He too had to get permission from his parents but foresaw no difficulty as his parents were also very supportive of his interests. He was also in his last term of school living close by his parents.

Attracted as they were to each other, it was too early perhaps for both of them to admit that they were growing into a romantic relationship as they were at the moment just enjoying each other's company and freedom of their maturing adulthood.

Unknown to both teenagers was the fact they were distantly related and that both sets of their parents were involved in a matter deeply imbedded in their ancestry.

-◇-

Part II

There was a time when meadow
grove and stream,
The earth and every common sight,
to me did seem
apparelled in celestial light,
The glory and the freshness of a dream.
It is not now as it hath been of yore;-
Turn wheresoever I may,
By night or day,
The things which I have seen I now
can see no more.

**—Ode Intimations of Immortality from
Recollections of Early Childhood
William Wordsworth (1804)**

Chapter 8
The Medici Lineage

Grace and her mother Maddy were descendants of the Zagel family, a branch of the Raimondine Dynasty, the Counts of Toulouse, that stemmed from the twelfth century in southern France. During the past 2000 years the family had been closely guarded by a Marechal designated by ancient beings. Malachi, or Michael as Maddy had known him, was the guardian of the sector of the Harmonic Universe within which Earth existed. This attention had safeguarded the conclusion of the Alignment leaving the planet now in a state of anticipation as to whether it would ascend.

Emerging from the Carolingian era the Counts of Toulouse originated as vassals of the Frankish Kings, ruling Toulouse and its surrounding region from the late ninth century until 1270.

As the Zagel family expanded throughout the Languedoc Roussillon and Catalan after the thirteenth century so did another lineage connected to the Counts of Toulouse.

Philippa d'Anduze inherited the Toulouse Dynasty from her relative, Countess Joan of Toulouse (1270). Unfortunately, through a slip up in the will the Dynasty and its lands were absorbed into the Roman Catholic Church and Crown Lands of France (Philip III) at that time.

This situation led to the family d'Anduze harbouring bitterness towards the Roman Catholic Church. Though they were not supporters of the Cathars they did allow themselves some empathy with regard to the persecution they experienced, though, in fact family members had informed the Inquisition of relatives who they believed supported the Cathar cause.[7]

In the thirteenth century the Halqu had tracked the Seal they were searching for to Southern France. They also knew that Philippa's soul, along with Maddy's, had been considered for the Alignment contract initially. When Maddy (Lilith) had been spirited away they turned their attention to Philippa and her lineage. They followed Philippa's incarnations and each time it drew them close to Maddy (Lilith) they had been thwarted, each time Lilith had escaped their clutches. Philippa's lineage from the outset had betrayed the knowledge of the Cloister of Lilith's contract.[8]

In the thirteenth century the bitterness of the family d'Anduze had led the Halqu to Malena, the then incarnation of Lilith. Thwarted, but pursuing Philippa's lineage, they had managed to track it down to the Court of the Medici in Florence and subsequently followed it to the Court of the King of France, Francois 1 and his descendants (sixteenth century).

-◇-

The genocide of the Cathars in the thirteenth century by the Roman Catholic Church and kings of France proved to have a shocking effect on Europe in general. It was the first appearance of the Inquisition which developed and spread throughout Europe. The Inquisition was a terrifying tool in the hands of the Church, subjugating the population by means of horrendous torture, imprisonment and burning at the stake. As with all situations extreme action produces a reaction and it was inevitable that this undercurrent of religious unrest would produce movements of protest.

In a very extreme way the example of Henry VIII's liaison and obsession for Anne Boleyn provided the catalyst which led to the reformation and creation of the Church of England. It was Anne Boleyn who introduced heretical literature, that of Calvin and Luther to Henry VIII. Anne had been a lady in waiting in the French court of Henri of Navarre's Queen Marguerite and it was probably there that she had learned of protestantism.

As in England at that time the Royal Court of France came under pressure from the same influences.

The Bible had become available in the many vernacular languages of France since the twelfth century and became the instigation of the Protestant movement. It could be said that since the genocide of the Cathars in the thirteenth century, it followed that the country had a long history of struggles with the Roman Catholic Church.

However, it was Jean Calvin (1509–1564, Swiss) theologian, who was the leading French Protestant reformer, influencing protestantism in France and elsewhere in Europe and thought to have had a major impact on the formation of the modern world.

-◇-

It was into this arena of political and religious turbulence that Catherine de Medici was thrust.

Her parents Lorenzo de' Medici (Duke of Urbino) and his wife Madeleine de la Tour d'Auvergne, the Countess of Boulougne, died within a month of her birth. Their marriage had been part of an alliance between King Francis 1 of France and Lorenzo's uncle Pope Leo X against the Holy Roman Emperor Maximilian 1.

King Francis had wanted Catherine to be raised in the French Court but Pope Leo placed her in the care of her paternal grandmother and then her aunt Clarice de Medici.

The Medici power was interrupted on the death of Pope Leo until the election of Pope Clement VII in 1523. Clement placed Catherine in the Palazzo Medici Riccardi in Florence where she became known by the Florentine people as 'duchessina', recognising her claim to the Duchy of Urbino.

In 1527 the Medici were overthrown in Florence and Catherine was taken hostage and placed in a succession of convents in which she was badly treated until she arrived at the final one, Santissima Annunzuata delle Murate, which she regarded as the happiest of times.

Clement eventually surrendered Florence to Charles, the Holy Roman Emperor and summoned Catherine to join him in Rome. It was then, at the age of 14 that she married Henri, the second son of King Francis and she entered the French Court. Henri, heavily involved with his governess, Diane de Poitiers since the age of 15 virtually ignored Catherine for the first ten years of their marriage. It was only on the death of his elder brother, the Dauphin, Francis, that the inheritance of the Royal House came into question and Henri began to pay attention to Catherine in the need to have an heir to the throne.

Henri and Catherine had many children, most feeble and sickly. She played a pivotal role in the lives of her sons who successively became young kings of France. Francis, her eldest son, married Mary, Queen of Scots, at which time the French Court was heavily ruled by the House of Guise. On Francis death Catherine became Queen Regent for her son Charles IX.

The duplicity of Catherine de Medici was evident in the way she exploited her authority; mainly balancing negotiations between the differing religious factors. One never knew where her allegiance lay, Catholic one minute and then supporting the Protestants next. Underlying all of this though was her intention of keeping the House of Valois on the Royal throne.

A force to be reckoned with she was named a 'poisonous serpent' due to her suspected poisoning of several people. Opposing her meant risking one's life by murder, poison or disappearance. Whether she deserved this evil reputation or not one should perhaps consider her upbringing and early adult hood in the hands of the French Court. Her personality was embittered due to Henri's devotion to his formidable mistress Diane de Poitiers, who virtually ruled the Paris court as queen. Catherine, young, became second to her husband's mistress's rule and her resentment towards her husband was fuelled.

Her most historic moment was being blamed for the massacre of St. Bartholomew's Eve, when thousands of Huguenots, Protestants were slain at the hands of the nobles, led by Charles IX and Francis, Duke de Guise.

Henry IV (the Bourbon King of Navarre, who eventually became King of France) said of Catherine:

I ask you, what could a woman do, left by the death of her husband, with five little children on her arms and two families of France who were thinking of grasping the crown – our own (the Bourbons) and the Guises? Was she not compelled to play strange parts to deceive first one and then the other, in order to guard, as she did, her sons, who successively reigned through the wise conduct of that shrewd woman? I am surprised that she never did worse.

-◇-

The eve of the feast of St Bartholomew the Apostle
August 23/24 1572

It was in this French Court that the Halqu hovering, watching, had discovered a descendent of Philippa d'Anduze. In doing so they also found the Seal they were searching for.

They found Maddy's soul embodied in the Royal family of Navarre. In this royal incarnation the Seal was Isabella Madeleine de Navarre a relative and lady in waiting to Queen Jeanne III of Navarre who was married to Antoine de Bourbon, Duke of Vendôme.

Jeanne was the acknowledged spiritual and political leader of the Protestant movement in France and a prominent figure in the French religious wars. Acknowledging publicly her allegiance to Calvinism she joined the Huguenots and negotiated a peace treaty with Catherine de Medici and arranged the marriage of her son, Henri to Catherine's daughter, Marguerite de Valois.

Isabella and her husband Louis had been summoned to Paris for this marriage of Queen Jeanne's son, Henri to

Marguerite, the sister of King's Charles IX. Louis was cousin to Henri. Many very prominent Huguenots had gathered in Paris, which was mainly Catholic, to attend the wedding.

-◇-

Isabella was nervously pacing the rooms allotted to her family. Word had percolated through the court that some really evil things were about to happen and as a Protestant she feared for the plight of her husband and their children.

It was imperative that they left immediately. The whispers that had permeated the inner court over previous days were that a major event would take place which would have a significant effect to the Protestants' presence in France. *What's going to happen,* thought Isabella. She felt her body trembling, fear overtaking her. Her place in Queen Jeanne's court had made her very aware of the unrest and threats to Protestants.

A soft tapping at the door alerted her to Michel, Louis's manservant who had come from the Louvre. He passed to her a message from her husband, telling her to gather her children and a few belongings and to meet him in the courtyard below. Doing as told she met her husband and Michel by a carriage. They pushed the family into the carriage and told Isabella that they would meet her later.

"Where are we going? What's happening?"

Glancing furtively around her husband responded.

"I have no time to tell you. Just do as I say. You are going to the port. Get on the ship that is waiting for you and I will join you there."

At that, he shouted to the carriage man to 'Go' without having the chance to make their farewells. The carriage sped out through the castle gate. As they travelled through the city there were crowds massing with flaming torches, people running backward and forward shouting. In the distance a great fire shot up following an explosion.

The carriage driver sped dangerously through the crowds until they reached the outskirts of the city, at which point he moderated his speed and shouted down to Isabella asking how the family were faring. Relief overcame Isabella as they left the city for the deserted countryside. After frequent stops for refreshment they arrived at the port the following evening and boarded the ship. Her husband was yet to appear.

Having put the children to bed in the bunks below, Isabella paced the deck through the night keeping watch for her husband. When dawn broke she saw horses approaching on the horizon and told the Captain of the ship to get ready to depart. As luck had it the weather was clement and the sea calm.

Her husband and followers arrived, jumping onto the ship and leaving their horses for the local stable men. Michel came and whispered to Louis.

"Louis, I must go now, return to Court or at least the city and send word of what has transpired."

Thanking him for his help and bidding him a safe journey Louis turned to Isabella and hustled her below deck, telling her the news of the great massacre of the Protestants that had taken place in Paris the previous evening. He was traumatised by what he had seen, hundreds of bodies, bloody and wounded, dead, lying in the streets and the Catholics scything their way through the city.

"Some say that it was the Queen, Catherine, who instigated the massacre, but Charles and his friend the Duke of Guise were seen frenziedly cutting down people. They began by murdering Admiral Coligny and other prominent leaders of the Huguenots. The way they were behaving they are not going to stop until they have murdered as many Protestants as they can find. That's why I decided we needed to get out."

Louis peered out of the port hole and to his relief saw that they had set sail and were well away from the French coastline.

"We will be safe in England. Elizabeth is a Protestant and has gained a lot of support. Hopefully we can gain some sympathy to our situation."

Arriving in England and after a brief sojourn in Queen Elizabeth's court Isabella and Louis and their family settled not far away.[9]

-◇-

Cateline was one of Catherine de Medici's servants working closely to the queen in her chambers. She was the illegitimate offspring of a liaison between King Henri II and a courtesan. She was brought up in a nursery on the outskirts of the castle; the nursery also had other illegitimate children with royal parentage, their parentage denied. They were made courtesans or servants, depending on the status of their mother, in the royal Court.

On the night of the massacre she was present in the chambers of the Queen Mother listening to the ranting between Catherine and her sons and the Duke of Guise. The King (Charles IX) was arguing with her, backed up by the

Duke de Guise. It seemed they were intent on ridding Paris of Protestants. Both were very drunk and neither was listening to the Queen Mother's pleas for moderation. Their main target seemed to be Admiral Gaspard de Coligny. They felt his death would send a message to all Protestants.

Cateline's closeness to the Queen Mother and the gossip she had heard had made her aware that the Queen Mother had a secret and close relationship with Coligny's son so she could understand why she was trying to calm the situation down. Coligny's father had brought Catherine de Medici to France from Italy and developed a close friendship with her during her first difficult years in France.

Listening to all of this frightened Cateline. Using an excuse to fetch more wine she left the chambers and scurried to the kitchen where she met her friend Pierre. She and Pierre had only recently become lovers. He was valet to Charles IX and she was deeply aware of his convictions. He often asked her what she had overheard in the Queen Mother's chambers and encouraged her to listen furtively.

Cateline was aware that he reported all the information gathered in his own work with the King and from her work with the Queen Mother to an agent of a rebel faction which neither sided with the Protestants or the Catholics but was working independently for its own purposes. Pierre saw it as a way to amass wealth and escape Court life in the future. However, the purposes of the rebel group proved mysterious to him.

Recently their conversations had revolved around the forthcoming marriage and the guests who would be invited. She had noted that Pierre had become increasingly interested in one of the guests closely related to Queen Jeanne of

Navarre, the mother of the bridegroom. She had told Pierre that Isabella de Navarre and her husband Louis would be arriving and where they would be staying, the apartments in the central part of the castle not far from the Queen Mother's chambers.

Pierre's interest in the woman had heightened recently, he asked Cateline for anything she knew about the wedding and where guests would be located. An uncanny sense told her that perhaps Isabella's life was threatened and that there was some plot to capture her and possibly, as she was a Protestant, kill her.

Cateline's prescience was correct. The agent Pierre reported to was Andre Chaput and it was he that reported to the Halqu and it was exactly their intention.

Michel, Louis' manservant, was actually Malachi and behind the scenes he had instigated the removal of the family, and importantly Isabella, to safety. Louis had been accepted into the 'Cloister of Lilith' as Isabella's guardian and had recently been told that he had to take Isabella to England for her safety.

Malachi stepped up to level 7, the place of reunion, to report to Nammu.

Nammu told him to return to Paris and search out the family betrayer as the Halqu had instigated the action in the hope of snatching Isabella. He wanted to know exactly what had happened to Isabella, who it would appear was safely on her way to England.

-◇-

Chapter 9
Return to France

(2013)

Grace was now seated on a flight on her way to Perpignan in France. The preceding week had been a flurry of organisation, leaving Jonah under the supervision of her husband and grandmother Madeleine.

She sipped the scalding hot sweet tea the stewardess had served, relaxing a little and thinking about the conversations she had had with her father. Grace had resolved her differences with him, mainly because he seemed genuinely concerned about her mother's disappearance. He had sent her a new mobile phone and, to her surprise, told her that he had decided he would follow her out to France in a few days' time. Grace was going to find somewhere to stay in the village near the 'Croft', the chalet belonging to her mother.

Having been to the Lake District to attempt to contact the Uncle Simon she had been told about had led nowhere and Grace somehow sensed that Simon too might have disappeared. He seemed to be a bit mysterious. Her grandmother Madeleine had not been able to tell her much about him other than that she had been very close to him in her youth but had lost touch until recently when he had contacted her and gone out to see Maddy in France. It was also a surprise as she told Grace that the chalet her parents had bought was the very same one her French great grandparents had lived in. Her grandmother had never previously spoken about her early life, or, in fact, revealed that she was French. She spoke perfect English without a trace of accent.

Looking out of the window she saw the Pyrenees on the horizon, the white peaks sparkling in the sunshine against a backdrop of a brilliant blue sky. Preparing herself for the landing she settled into her seat, wondering at how relaxed she actually felt while at the same time there was a prickling sense of anticipation coursing through her.

-◇-

As her mother had felt before, driving up through the Tet Valley towards the mountains, she too felt a strange connection with the landscape. It was an easy drive through beautiful countryside, some parts of which revealed sandy cliffs with strange shapes uncannily like figures struggling into some kind of form. There was not much traffic on the roads and Grace found herself comparing the lack of traffic to the overwhelmingly crowded roads of England. She wended her way up through the valleys to the higher mountains and arrived late morning in the village beyond Borg Madame. Feeling hungry she decided to find a cafe for lunch; afterwards she would find somewhere to stay. Spotting a cafe on the corner of the square she headed over to it having parked her car nearby. Glancing around she saw there were not many people about.

Grace headed for a table on the edge of the terrace, taking her jacket off, the day was getting really hot, she pulled out a chair and sat down. Apart from a couple of men seated at a table nearby there were no other customers.

A girl came out and Grace ordered a cafe au lait. She threw her head back, her face to the sun and drank in the heady fresh air that carried the hint of coffee and a spicy tang of herbs from the gardens below. She was used to the polluted air of her local town; this was like having a shot of adrenalin and she felt herself reviving.

The coffee arrived and glancing around she smiled at the men at the nearby table. Thirsty, she gulped the coffee and caught the waitress's eye and ordered another. As the waitress set the coffee down she asked if there was a chambre d'hote in the village and was told there was a gallery around the corner that also offered bed and breakfast. Grace followed this by asking whether she knew of the Croft and was given directions.

-◇-

From their table at 'Les Guingettes' the two men that Grace had noticed as she sat down, had spotted her heading towards the cafe and exchanged a glance, raising their eyebrows. They had been eavesdropping on the conversation Grace was having with the waitress and as the waitress returned to the bar Simon got up and approached Grace.

"Did I hear you mention the Croft?"

"Yes." Surprised, Grace turned towards Simon.

"Sorry, but we weren't listening intentionally. We know the Croft very well and we know your mother."

"You know my mother?"

Simon sat down by Grace.

"Yes, I had better introduce myself. Simon Zagel, you may have heard of me. I am the cousin of your grandmother, Madeleine."

Grace's surprise was turning to shock at so quickly coming face to face with her distant relative and the possibility of finding out about her mother.

"Oh my God, Granny and I have been trying to contact you. She knew that you were in France but had no address or telephone number for you here."

"Yes, that was rather remiss of me…however…"

Grace butted in.

"We have been so worried about Mum. Where is she? Do you know?"

"Yes."

"Is she here?" Grace, agitated, was looking around.

"She is safe and well but we need, that is my colleague and I, need to spend time with you to explain what has happened. Are you staying nearby?"

"I have only just arrived and was about to look for accommodation."

"Well, don't worry, I have the keys to the Croft and I know your mother would want you to stay there. When you've finished your coffee perhaps we could drive up there with you and settle you in. And then we need to talk." Simon finished on a firm note.

"Very well, but having only just met you I am feeling apprehensive. You sound very mysterious and you are expecting me to accept you, how do I know you are who you say you are and who is your colleague?"

Grace glanced across to the other man; Malachi was still seated at the nearby table.

"Let me show you my passport and if you have a mobile we could call you grandmother if that would reassure you?"

Simon took out his passport and handed it to her. Grace took out the new iPhone that her father had bought her and rang her grandmother.

"Granny, I have just arrived here and driven into the square near Mum's house. There are two men here who say they know her and what has happened to her. One of them is Simon. Can you speak to him and reassure me he is who he says he is? It has all come at me too quickly. He says he is going to explain what has happened to her."

Grace handed the telephone to Simon and saw him having a very relaxed conversation with her grandmother. He handed the phone back to her, smiling.

"Hello."

"That's Simon, you are perfectly safe with him. Trust him, I am sure he will be able to reassure us about Maddy. Speak to me soon and let me know what's happening."

Closing her phone, Grace stood up, still feeling apprehensive and said.

"I feel I can relax a bit now, shall we go up to Mum's? I am intrigued."

Simon and Malachi went to their car which was parked not far from Grace's hire car and indicated for her to follow them.

-◇-

Chapter 10
Maddy Meets Grace at the 'Croft'

(France, 2013)

Back at the 'Croft' Maddy felt a heaviness cloak her as she reduced her vibration down to three dimensions. She thought, *now I know what Malachi must have endured*. Trying to settle down she walked to the door and saw Simon and Michael walking up the pathway, followed by Grace. She wondered how she was going to start to explain everything to Grace. They saw her and called out a greeting.

"Mum – is it you? It's so good to see you, we have been so worried."

"I'm sorry, darling, come in, let's settle down and I will try to explain. Perhaps we should have a drink; coffee, tea?"

Maddy looked questioningly at Malachi and Simon, silently asking for their help.

"I'll make some tea," Simon offered and went over to the kitchen area and switched on the kettle.

Pausing, waiting for the tea, Maddy turned to Grace.

"How's your father?" she asked.

"Well, not good. Diana has left him, seems he has repeated his usual behaviour, you know, you put up with it. She is a feminist and when he started to get buried in the project and they hardly saw each other she gave him the shove."

How ironical, Maddy thought to herself. She felt the comparison of her three-dimensional incarnation bouncing off her ancestral soul heritage.

"Do you want to see him? He has asked after you and seemed genuinely concerned?"

The question hung in the air. There was a brief interlude when Simon came over with the tea and a quiet descended on the party.

"Where have you been?"

Maddy rose and went to the window not knowing how to begin to tell her daughter of her experience.

"Grace, I know that what I am about to tell you may seem spectacularly weird; it did to me at first but the more Simon and Michael explained to me, the more I became aware. Something in me told me I had been on some track for eons – it felt right, it felt like a fundamental truth that I had to face. Please be patient and let me explain."

Maddy looked to Simon and he nodded. She then told Grace about the events of the last few years and of the Alignment – how she had learned about her role and explained the aspects of reincarnation of her soul.

Grace's initial astonishment turned to disbelief and she began to think her mother had gone crazy.

"I can't believe all that stuff. You aren't having a…" The question hanging in the air.

"Whatever you are about to say, don't. No, I am perfectly fine, it is just that the last year has been, how can I put it, intense."

"But what are you telling me? Who are you then?"

"We are called Ancients; we are ascended into a soul existence that is outside the concepts of three-dimensional existence such as you and this planet's experience. We choose to take on a task, a role for the good of all. It is part of our soul's journey and the part I played in the Alignment was a task that I chose. In the timeline you know it was in the region of Sumeria, that is where Iraq and Iran are now, some 8,500 years ago. To reach the time of the Alignment I had to experience life on Earth, so it has been a very long journey through many incarnations."

"And the role you played, it's finished now?"

"Yes and no. In this incarnation I had to become aware of who I was, am, and my obligations. It took time to raise my frequency, that is to reinstate my powers as an ancient which involves interdimensional and time travel. Now the process has started, it has accelerated and I am realising and returning to my soul state."

"What does that mean?"

"It means that I have to make a choice, return to my soul state, remain here in this three-dimensional existence with you and the family or enlist into another task but for the moment I can't. I have to come to terms with what has happened and I can only do that here and with the help of my mentors."

"You mean here at 'the Croft'?"

"Yes, and also somewhere else." Maddy hesitated to explain where else.

Grace was struck dumb and there was a marked pause in their conversation. After a few minutes Grace asked, "What about the family? Are you going to come back to us?"

"I don't know. It depends, as I just told you. I am sorry this must be very difficult for you to follow. How you are seeing me...perhaps as a stranger?" Maddy faltered...

Grace was beginning to feel angry, mainly due to the worry she had been going through and she perceived somehow that her mother might abandon the family and she was at a loss to understand what was going on. Trying to ground the conversation she threw in.

"Dad's coming out tomorrow."

"Why?" Maddy asked, stupefied.

"He is concerned about you."

"Bit late for that, isn't it?"

Grace, seeing a bit of her old mum said, "Come on, he is sorry and wants to help sort things out."

"You have to understand things have changed, I have changed. I know it sounds unbelievable but for the time being, I must ask for your understanding and allow me to sort myself out. I don't want to make a rash decision."

Maddy was beginning to feel pressured and looked towards Michael for help.

"Perhaps we could call on Nammu?" he said, looking at Simon thoughtfully.

"Well, that would be a first for me too having never met him." Simon murmured.

-◇-

Maddy had moved out onto the terrace for fresh air and a chance to gather her thoughts. Michael followed her.

"Grace is obviously having a problem with all of this; too much too soon. Simon and I are thinking that perhaps we need to call in some help from Nammu."

"What do you mean?"

"Well, Nammu, an Ancient, such as yourself, would give some credence to your story. He will also be able to access her DNA and help her to understand."

"I think it may be a good idea but I am concerned. It has been already a lot for her to take in, the same as it was for me and I had time with Pam to wake up."

"Trust me, she has your DNA and will understand. She will wake up just as you have. She also has a contract that she took out for this incarnation to fulfil. Anyway, let's see what happens. I have summoned him and he is bringing Isolde with him."

They returned to the room which now felt different. The light intensified and Nammu appeared in the room followed by Isolde in her human form. Isolde instantly changed to her cat form and went over and sat at Grace's feet. Grace nearly dropped her cup on seeing the change in Isolde.

Nammu was conventionally dressed for the times in jeans, lightweight tweed jacket, shirt with cravat, looking the part of an English country gentleman.

He walked over to Grace who seemed to be in shock. Isolde jumped onto Grace's lap and started nestling and padding on her stomach. Grace automatically put her hand out to stroke her. Seeing Nammu advance Isolde jumped down as Grace rose. Nammu took her hand.

"Who are you?" Grace exclaimed.

"Hello, Grace, let me introduce myself. My name is Nammu, more formally Overseer Fraterne Nammu. Your mother told you that she was an Ancient, we thought perhaps you should meet me as I am one also."

"But how did you get here and from where?"

"Our existence is a little difficult to understand from your current perspective. Earth has yet to reach the scientific and technological development equivalent, although probably in 700 years' time it will have caught up. However, in the meantime let me explain a little to you."

"We can exist in many dimensions and time travel in the universe as a whole. Having ascended to be ancients we help other universes. Each universe is tuned into frequencies thereby producing multifarious planetary evolutions. There are many so called Harmonic Universes as everything exists through sound, music and diverse frequencies."

"Our role is to help, guide these universes by ascension back to Source, that is the Creator of All. You may think of it as God but that is too simplistic. Creator of all or Prime Mover is an abstract entity from which all life emanates, not by control but by evolving, that is the fittest survive, the weakest fade away as circumstances intervene and change things."

"But why are you here now?" asked Grace.

"Currently the Earth is going through a crucial time in its evolution. The situation is very grave. It was because of this time that we knew was coming that your mother, to give her ancient name, Lilith, was contracted to go to the relevant time to guard your family line to the point of Alignment. I think the Alignment has been explained to you?"

Grace nodded, bewildered. She turned to Michael and Simon.

"Are you ancients too?"

Michael replied, "No, I am a Marechal, and not as ascended as the ancients or your mother. I was given this sector, that is Earth, the Galaxy and universe of which they are part to guard as a stage in my path to ascend back to Source. You know me as Michael but my name is Malachi. My guardianship intensified during the approach of the Alignment as your mother was in danger of being abducted by the Halqu."

Grace interrupted.

"The Halqu?"

"Yes, they are an extra-terrestrial species that have been pursuing your mother, the other Seals and the Shield through time."

Grace turned to Simon quizzically…Simon added, "I am purely your mother's guardian on Earth at this time. I was sworn into the Cloister of Lilith when I was 20 years old to guard your grandmother, Madeleine, as she was the Seal then and passed it on to your mother."

"Stop!" exclaimed Grace.

"I need time to take this in, you have introduced so many things into our conversation that I can't keep up and I don't understand. I need time with my mother, this is totally bizarre. I can see that you have enormous powers, obviously slipping in and out of…what…dimensions, time?"

She looked at Malachi and Nammu…

"Obviously you are extra-terrestrial beings and your existence way beyond what anybody on earth at the moment would believe."

Looking sceptically towards her mother Grace murmured, "I need time with Mum. I am having difficulty in understanding who my mother is, the one I knew. Let alone the rest of it! Let me have some time." Grace near to tears implored.

The party looked from one to the other and acknowledged the situation. Nammu took Malachi aside.

"We have done enough for the time being. It will sink in," Nammu said.

"I will stay for the time being and take Simon down to the village and stay with him."

Grace stared intensely at Nammu as he bade farewell to everyone stating, as he walked towards the hallway and dissolved into the surroundings.

"All time, all things are now and complete."

Isolde who had been sitting on an armchair asleep, roused and noting that Nammu had disappeared, leapt up, rubbed against Malachi's legs and headed for the hallway, and in doing so changed into her human form. Glancing back over her shoulder she smiled at everyone and disappeared.

Grace by this time was speechless.

Malachi said to Simon, "Let's leave Maddy and Grace alone."

Turning to them he said, "We will come back tomorrow and see how you are."

"Yes, that's a good idea," said Maddy.

As Malachi and Simon left Maddy turned to Grace, who by this time was looking exhausted.

"I am so sorry, Grace, you just need to adjust to everything."

"Let's have something to eat and rest and then we can talk."

-◇-

Later Grace was sitting with her mother, Maddy holding her hand.

"I am so sorry, Grace, but you did need to understand as you are part of all of this."

"What do you mean?"

"As Nammu told you the Earth and its population are passing through an evolutionary stage. It is in grave danger of not surviving."

"You mean we might be wiped out."

"Yes. You don't remember but you need to wake up. Before you were born, like everyone, you contracted to carry out a certain role during your lifetime. Yours was to assist at this time."

"You are quite right, I don't remember."

"You will…in the events that are unfolding, it will become clear to you. In the meantime, rest, try to digest what you have been told and trust that all will be well."

"Dad's arriving tomorrow, are we going to have to tell him all of this as well?"

"It depends."

-◇-

Maddy was left contemplating. Colin was coming out, it would be the first time they would be together since his affair. *How was it going to be?* Maddy thought to herself.

Reflecting on their marriage she felt it had been good in all aspects, shared interests and of course the children, but then, Diana appeared on the scene.

Maddy's incarnations through the period of her contract had necessitated her being involved in the physical relations the Earthlings engaged in. Now this was all over and she was returning to her ancient existence she could reflect objectively on the many relationships, marriages she had had through her lives on Earth.

She noted the major characteristics of the Earthlings were their strong aggressive and sexual instincts.

This last incarnation had particularly demonstrated this to her. The majority of the population on Earth were struggling to cover their basic living requirements. In response the aggressive traits were heightened; an increase in murders, youths fighting and killing each other, rape and sexual perversion. Technology and social media had not helped, the population was able to access all things to satisfy their aggressive needs.

Reflecting on her many incarnations as an Earthling, she realised she had been subject to these urges, admitting to herself that some of it she had enjoyed but also been terrified by some very violent experiences.

Now she was happy to leave this behind and return to her elevated soul level where intimacy between souls was of mind union. It was an ecstatic experience but something bothered her about her memories of the physical contact she had experienced on Earth and the empathy shared with chosen partners.

Maddy jolted and came too, feeling the sensations of her reverie and feeling frustrated, human being frustrated, and then regret at the sense of loss that remained in her soul of the physical experience.

She also realised that from the Earth point of view relationships were enacted within the culture of the religion's accepted form and as such she sensed how the population on

Earth was seething with unrequited love and frustration, not able to achieve their individual potential due to social restrictions.

How did this leave her and her relationship with Colin, did she want to get back with him in this Earth incarnation?

As things transpired Colin did not come out to France.

-◇-

Chapter 11
Granny Madeleine

Grace was struggling, due to her mother's behaviour. Having found her safe she had felt a sense of relief. The anxiety of the past months lifted. However what was disturbing Grace was the fact that she felt she did not know who her mother was. It was as if she was confronted with a complete stranger on the one hand and the mother she knew was but a shadow skirting this new person.

What was also deeply troubling was all the information she was having to digest from her mother backed up by her cousin Simon. Not only that, but people were materialising out of thin air which was even more disturbing. At the moment her credulity was stretched to breaking point.

Sitting at the cafe sipping her coffee with her hands wrapped comfortingly around the warm ceramic, she let herself go and slumped back into the chair. She felt events were out of her control and reluctantly began to see the best approach was to live moment by moment.

Looking up she saw her mother and Simon approaching.

"We have some unfortunate news," her mother began.

"Granny fell over and has been taken to hospital. The carer found her on her morning call. They don't know how long she had been lying there. She was very cold and barely breathing, the shock of the fall probably. At the moment she is stable but they are reviewing her situation. However, they have advised us to go back as soon as possible so perhaps it is more serious."

Grace looked to her mother and Simon and saw the gravity of the situation in their faces.

"Okay, let's see if we can get on a flight later today."

Grace felt a foreboding that even further turmoil was looming.

-◇-

They were lucky, the three managed to get a flight out of Perpignan that evening and on arrival decided to go straight to the hospital. Unfortunately they were just too late. Madeleine died an hour before they arrived. Going in to see her they were at least presented with a comforting memory they could hold on to. The staff told them that they had put her on end of life care earlier that afternoon.

Propped up on pillows in the comfortable room Madeleine looked as if she were merely dozing peacefully, a smile on her face and her colour looking as if she were going to open her eyes and greet them.

Maddy wiped her tears away and turned to Grace putting her arm around her. Simon was quiet but Grace could see he was holding back his emotions and was very tense.

The nursing staff handed Maddy Madeleine's possessions. They all went to Grace's house as it was the nearest. Going through the possessions Maddy came across a locket of her mother's. Feeling the loss of her mother she put the locket on as a way of comforting herself.

-◇-

With the shock of Madeleine dying and everything else that was going on they decided to call a family conference immediately after the funeral.

Refreshments were served in Madeleine's house after the interment. When the mourners had left, the family congregated in the sitting room. Maddy and Colin and her brother Charlie gathered alongside Simon, Grace and her brothers David and Mark who had flown in from Cambodia. Jonah was also there.

The family solicitor had turned up with a bundle of papers. Everybody was very quiet and really not knowing what to say. The solicitor went through the terms of the will which was very simple, Madeleine had left everything to Maddy and Charlie in equal shares.

Maddy glanced around her mother's sitting room and realised the task ahead. It looked like a museum, full of old vases and ornaments, mirrors and Persian rugs on the floor. Very much her mother's generation. Comfortable, country and affluent. What were they going to do with everything! Of interest too was mention of the bank vault and its contents. Maddy had relinquished the Collar to Simon at the time of the Alignment but knew that there was a ring belonging to her grandfather that should go to her brother Charlie. Turning to Charlie she said.

"We must go to the bank tomorrow and find out what is in it. I have no idea other than I know grandfather had a ring that had been passed down to him which I think must be very valuable."

Charlie nodded and they agreed on a time and meeting place for the following day. General discussion ensued and Colin, very good at organising was given the task of going through Madeleine's house with Maddy and Charlie and agreeing how to deal with the contents. He was the perfect person to take charge as his mother had died the previous year and he had dealt with her estate very swiftly which had been a great relief to the family as it was an arduous task. Having made the decisions they dispersed, agreeing to meet the following evening and report progress.

-◇-

Maddy and Charlie went to the bank and were led to the vaults. The manager opened their mother's box and placed it in a private viewing room. Both were astonished to see a heavy folder full of notes and writing. Underneath was a small box containing a ring wrapped in a small piece of soft leather. Maddy was intrigued.

"It's the same symbol as the one on the collar and also in the window of the building lower down in the garden at The Croft."

Touching the locket at her neck she looked down and saw the same symbol engraved on it.

"It's peculiar, I didn't really notice the engraving on this locket but it is the same."

Charlie had been leafing through the folder and said dismissively stepping aside.

"It looks like a lot of nonsense to me."

Maddy started turning the pages and saw mention of the Cathars and the Counts of Toulouse and there were some very ancient documents that looked like genealogy trees.

Turning to her brother she said.

"Do you want any of these? The ring obviously is yours as I had the Collar that Mother gave me on my 21st birthday."

"No, I have enough possessions and don't want to add to it. I have no one to pass the ring on to so perhaps we should leave it here for your children. At least it's safe here. You can have the folder too."

"Well, if you are sure."

Maddy collected the papers and decided that she would go through everything with Simon when she got back to France.

-◇-

Returning to Madeleine's house they met Colin who had been going through their mother's belongings. He summed up his findings to Maddy and Charlie.

"There are some objects d'art which I think should go to an auction house as they are probably very valuable. I also came across a quantity of jewellery which I haven't touched."

"Perhaps you should go through it together and decide what to do with it. The furniture and other items, well again it is all very good quality and some pieces need to go to an auction house."

"If you want me to I will get in touch with one tomorrow and get somebody out to look at everything. That is, after you have decided what to keep. Perhaps I am going too fast, just let me know what you want me to do. Tom's desk has been left exactly as it was after he died so it is going to take time but you should go through it. There may be insurance policies or other items of value. I didn't go through anything of that nature."

Maddy and Charlie were sitting quietly. They decided to have a day to absorb events as everything had moved along rapidly since their mother had died. Maddy found herself musing over the contents of the vault box and trying to link the artifacts, the Collar, locket and the ring and her grandfather's interest in the genealogy of his family. Her brain was making connections.

-◇-

Chapter 12
Family History

The family finally dealt with Madeleine's estate. It had taken two weeks which was quick considering the prolific contents of the house. The house sold quickly and the conveyancing and probate were in process and taking the usual amount of time.

The family knew this would probably take 3–6 months. Satisfied that there was no more to do other than wait they all sat down together over a meal to discuss moving on. Conversation was subdued, Maddy was feeling exhausted. Charlie was not much help as he lived in a very self contained bubble unaware of the toll it took on family members to clear up the estate.

Maddy's son, Mark, had told her he was returning to Cambodia, and David, her other son was back at work in the City. Both were unaware of her situation in France with Nammu and Malachi. She hoped that she might not have to involve them. They were good sons and she knew they would help if need be.

Grace had been thinking deeply about her mother and questioned Maddy as to her plans for the future.

Maddy said that before she returned to France she wanted to go through her father's desk and papers. She had already started and had come across a manuscript. It seemed in rather a rudimentary form, lots of notes inserted into the text. She was finding it very interesting and it seemed predominantly to be referring to the area in France where the Croft was.

Grace took a call from her husband, Richard. After the call she told Maddy that Jonah was asking if he might go to a meeting in the local town. He had developed an interest in astronomy and had joined a Stargazing Club. The meeting the following night involved him being up most of the night with a group from the club so that they could observe the constellations. The forecast was good for a clear sky.

Grace was amused.

"It seems Jonah has a girlfriend."

Maddy said, "He's a bit young for that, isn't he?"

"Not really, though perhaps I should have said that she is a special friend which is how he described her. He was keen however. We agreed of course and Richard is going to drop him off at the place and pick him up in the morning."

"Do you know who she is?"

"She goes to the local private boarding school at St Albans. They allow the senior girls to go out at the weekends into the town and that's where Jonah and his friends first met her, in one of the coffee shops. Her name is Philippa Andrews."

"Nice name," said Maddy but was somewhat disturbed recalling a faint memory. Musing she let it go for the moment wondering whether she had come across the name in the manuscript she had found in the vault. Perhaps her grandfather had traced the family back and it included some reference in his notes or the manuscript.

Having resolved to go through the documents thoroughly with Simon on her return to France she thought that in the meantime until her flight, she would sift through the papers and get them into some sort of order.

Grace left to see Richard and Jonah before they went off to the meeting. Maddy decided to go back to Colin's apartment and take all the papers collected from her father's desk and spend a day on them. She was feeling strange; somehow there was a connection between the papers and her recent plight. Also the name of Jonah's friend had unsettled her. She felt something was working outside on her peripheral existence and moving towards another…what?

She was also feeling a tug coming from Malachi and Nammu, as if on some level they were trying to get her to contact them. And what about Magda and Grace, should they meet, and for what purpose?

Making their farewells and promises to meet again soon the family parted and went their separate ways. Maddy went to Madeleine's house and boxed up her parents' papers and took them to Colin's apartment. It was a small apartment but Colin had cleared a space in a spare room which had a desk where he did his paper work.

"This should do, how long do you think it is going to take? We need to talk about what we are going to do once you have finished. Are you going back to France?"

"For the time being yes, I have made a life for myself there and there are quite a few things to tie up regarding recent events as you know. What are you going to do?"

"I feel at a loose end, my job with Chris came to an end recently which was quite good as it cut the tie with Diana. It was becoming embarrassing when we met at work after we split. She became rather vitriolic," Colin said this in a low tone, his voice petering out.

"Would you consider letting me come out to see you in France? I know it is a bit of a cheek to ask considering what has happened."

"I need to think about it but I don't see why not. We need to sort out a few issues first and perhaps Simon would let you stay with him in the village. I know he would be willing to help us and I also know that he is staying on there for a time."

-◇-

Chapter 13
Grandfather Jack's Notes

Having returned to France, Maddy and Simon sifted through the documents of her father, Tom, which were integrated into those of her grandfather Jack's research. Jack had traced his family, the Gills, back to the thirteenth century, to a supposed monk who had fled to the local abbey from the persecution in France. The monk's name was Tomas Lamberte de St Gilles and it seemed that probably he was a knight, not a monk.

Jack had summised that this knight had married, and following the genealogy it was his descendants that resulted in the present Gill family. He had also noted that the symbol on the ring he had inherited was probably the family symbol of the St Gilles.

Jack's notes were extensive. Spreading them out on the floor they saw his intention had been to trace the genealogy of the St Gilles who were connected to the Counts of Toulouse and the vast Ramoindine Dynasty. The family of St Gilles was one of the most powerful in Europe and regarded as the equals of kings. They were related to the Royal houses of England, France and Aragon.

Maddy's father had attached a note stating that names and titles were interchangeable in the middle ages so the family may have been called 'de St Gilles' or 'de Toulouse'. They originated from the town of St Gilles, present day in the Carmargue which at the time was a major commercial centre and converged two pilgrim routes to Compestela.

Maddy exclaimed, "Tomas Lamberte was a Knight Templar of the '*Ordre du Temple*' or 'The Poor Fellow-Soldiers of Christ and of the Temple of Solomon', originally formed by the church as a Christian military order to provide warriors for the Crusades. Look here," she continued by quoting from the notes...

The Counts of Toulouse were the first rulers to establish European foundations for both the Knights Templars and Knights Hospitaliers.

"Jack is obviously making the connection. From our point of view though, Tomas was most probably the knight in the legend who brought the princess to the Croft in the thirteenth century, a previous incarnation of mine, Malena."

Simon had been quietly reading more of Jack's notes.

"I can understand why she had to be spirited away if she was connected to this family."

and he read out.

...at the time of the Cathar persecution the Counts of Toulouse were model rulers. Far more liberal and tolerant than their more conventionally Catholic peers declining to discriminate against Jews, Cathars or other religious dissidents...

...learning and literacy flourished, women enjoyed greater freedom and the culture of the troubadours and courtly love created and encouraged...

...cities were allowed to set up municipal governments... with democratically elected consuls.

All of this innovative activity invited the condemnation of the Roman Church, ultimately causing a religious war, the fall of the House of Toulouse and extinction of their line...

...despite this the St Gilles family never lost the respect of the people of the Languedoc. Both Ramon VI and Ramon VII had been publicly humiliated, stripped, flogged and excommunicated. Yet...people still flocked to kiss the hems of their robes. It is perhaps an echo of this respect that their heraldic device may still be seen everywhere that they ruled 800 years ago.

Simon, having finished reading fell silent, contemplating the fact that people often referred to the Cathar cross but that it was, originally, the shield of the Counts of Toulouse.

"No wonder the monk fled France if he was a relative. What a prestigious and humanitarian family for their age. But does this link with your and Mum's family the Zagels and Jack's the Gill family!" exclaimed Maddy.

"Well, look here," Simon said pointing to a genealogical tree that Jack had mapped out.

"See, Tomas Lamberte is here and you can see his father was a Count of St Gilles, which makes him part of this dynasty. Tomas had a brother Ramon and there is a daughter, Madeleine Raymonde, his only offspring. But there seems to be no further trace of her. The line stops there as it does for Thomas."

Maddy interjected, "If they were persecuted as suggested, are you thinking what I am thinking?"

"Yes, Malena, Madeleine Raymonde is the Princess in the Legend. But we know that; this is physical proof."

Maddy continued, "They had to hide her as she carried the song. She had to survive and she must have done because the legend survived and the family. You and Mum are descendants as am I. There is a long and complicated history here. Incredible that it has survived. With all that I now know, from the Alignment, remembering my soul history, and the dreams and regressions I have had, I see how I came to the Croft. There are many people I have met that I know have been with me through my incarnations, some to protect me obviously in their discreet way. So Mum and Dad are actually cousins, distant. Is it incestuous?" Maddy asked,

"I'm not quite sure how it works. I know that for royalty to marry other royals they have to have seven generation gaps. There has been far more than that in your parents case."

"We are all descended from this Ramoindine Dynasty with the line supposedly ending in the thirteenth century with Malena, Madeleine Raymonde. So the Dynasty didn't die out, we are the living proof of it, not just the memory. Tomas's job obviously was to secure the continuance of the true inheritance of the Counts of Toulouse."

Simon had returned to studying Jack's notes and remarked.

"Jack traced another lineage however from the same period, this one, look."

Running his finger over the genealogical tree he noted.

"This line are descendants too, of Count Raymond VI who was exiled to England due to the persecution of the Cathars, see, the line goes," and reading from Jack's notes:

Count of Toulouse VI married Jeanne, sister of Richard and John, (children of Henry II and Eleanor of Aquitaine). Their son became Raymond VII, whose daughter Joan married Alphonse, Count of Poitiers, brother of King Louis IX of France. He was brought up in the French Court and had no sympathy for Occitan culture or the Cathars and did nothing to prevent the persecution of the Cathars by the Inquisition.

"They had no children and Joan should have passed the Toulouse inheritance to the nearest male relative but she didn't, she passed it to the nearest female relative, Philippa de Lomagne, daughter of Marie d'Anduze, eldest daughter of Pierre Bermond VI d'Anduze, eldest son of Constance of Toulouse, eldest half-sister of Raymond VII (Joan's father)."

"Strikes me, it is a complicated family but all within the Ramoindine Dynasty and very strong connections with royalty."

"Wait a minute though." Simon still reading…

"Joan's will was invalidated and the lands and title were absorbed into the Papal See due to a clause in the will of Alphonse (Joan's husband) giving his wife's lands to the Comtate Vernaissin to the Holy See which was allowed and it became Papal territory, a status that it retained until 1791."

"After the French Revolution!" Maddy exclaimed.

"Yes, but his notes don't say anything about regaining land. The trail seems to have ended in 1791."

-◇-

Having made as much sense as they could of Jack's notes and her father's additions, Maddy and Simon identified two strands of the Ramoindine Dynasty running down from the twelfth century. One strand related to the Cathars and the other to the Roman Catholic Church.

From recent experience, putting all the evidence together, they were alarmed to realise that the extra-terrestrial visitors, the Halqu, were connected to the Roman Catholic persecution of heretical groups including the genocide of the Cathars in the twelfth century. This put an entirely different perspective on the Church's involvement. It was at that time that the Ramoindine Dynasty had faded out.

Maddy asked, "What was the name of the last descendant of the Counts of Toulouse?"

"Philippa de Lomagne, connected to the family of d'Anduze."

"Where is that?"

"It's over in the east of France towards the Alps. Jack has traced the family too, but only to the eighteenth century where it seems to have become very complex. Their name then was Lomagne."

"I know I am making some improbable connections but with the way the Alignment unfolded, perhaps not. Jonah's girlfriend's name is Philippa."

Simon responded, "This family seems to have been at the forefront of a significant amount of English history. See, here in the seventeenth century. The family was prominent against Cromwell and later on, again in France their name crops up again during the Huguenot uprising, which would perhaps point to their being descendants of Catholic sympathisers."

Referring again to the genealogical tree he continued, "Here is another tree, that of Eleanor of Provence. She was married to Henry III who was the son of King John which links us back into the Dynasty, she was sympathetic to the Cathars; the research is a bit sketchy but it does seem to have begun making links."

Picking this up Maddy said, "It would be interesting to see where this family is today. You know, from all that has happened to me there are alarm bells going off in my head with regard to Jonah's girlfriend. What do you think?"

Thoughtfully Simon replied, "I know what you mean but it's a very chance and remote connection if what you are saying is that Philippa is reincarnated and a descendent of Philippa of Anduze. However, losing their land and titles in the thirteenth century, would perhaps have been a very sore point for their descendants. Despite their views regarding the Cathars it could have fired up antipathy towards the Church and it would have been of interest to the Halqu to use them."

Maddy picked up the phone, "I am going to ring Grace and see if I can find out more about Philippa, perhaps suggest we could meet her."

"Hi, Grace, how are you?"

There was a short pause, Maddy listening as Grace filled her in on the latest news.

"Oh, how interesting, I was going to ask how Jonah is getting on with Philippa. You say it is more serious now?"

Grace replied, "Yes, her father has asked to meet Jonah, invited him to their Country Estate."

Bemused, Maddy repeated, "Country estate?"

"Yes his family name is Andrews. He is a Lord and obviously inherited the estate, it sounds as if it is a very old family. They have acres of land, a huge mansion, you can picture it, can't you? Like Downton Abbey."[10]

Maddy sensed Grace was smiling, amused at the situation.

"Yes, I see," Maddy responded cautiously.

"He has extended the invitation to all of us, you included. It has made me feel that their relationship has become more serious and that her father is checking the situation out. What do you think? I am having a few qualms about it, Jonah is only 17 years old."

"Come on, Grace, you and Richard were in you first year at university when you met."

"Okay, but it seems different when he is your only child. Do you think you and Simon could come with us? It would be a great support to go as a family. It feels a bit daunting."

"When is it?"

"Two weeks' time. We are invited to arrive on Friday afternoon, spend Saturday there and leave after lunch on the Sunday. It could be a lovely weekend break for you. Anyway, think about it and ring me back and I will make the arrangements for you both."

Putting the phone down Maddy relayed the news to Simon.

"This all seems too coincidental, I sense Nammu and Malachi are setting things up, don't you? And one has to wonder for exactly what! Perhaps other forces are in play."

Simon considered.

"Well, it would give us an opportunity to meet Philippa's family."

Simon was now pacing up and down, weighing up the situation and considering what to say.

"Tell you what, I'll contact my friends in the Service, they will do some research on Lord Andrews for me."

Maddy musing.

"Oh, Simon, that would be helpful. It would give us some background and what we should be looking out for."

"We should meet Malachi and Nammu," Simon said gazing preoccupied down onto the garden of the Croft noting that the black cat was toying with a mouse on the terrace.

His thoughts were taking him to the line of betrayals that had followed Maddy's family down through history. He was wondering whether these relatives, or rather descendants and thereby relatives of Philippa of Lomagne, were the line of betrayers.

In which case if they were they had a strong grudge against Maddy's ancestors and extended family.

This may have made them vulnerable to the Halqu's cause. The Halqu may well have been able to use this vengeful attitude for their own purpose.

"Mmmmm," Simon muttered. "Looks like Isolde is back. Perhaps we could send her with a message. I'll go now and get on with that. Let me know dates for flying back and arrangements for when we get there. In the meantime I will get in touch with Malachi and let him know what's happening."

Ironically Simon added, "I am sure he can fill in many of the gaps."

Maddy laughed. "Yes, this does feels a bit too coincidental. Something is afoot that they, the Ancients, need us to do."

"Looks like it," Simon said, waving to her and heading off down the path to the village.

-◇-

From the console on the POD Nammu and Malachi were aware of Simon and Maddy's research. They look at each other.

At that moment Isolde materialised next to them.

"About time to make a few explanations I think," said Nammu.

-◇-

Chapter 14
Return to the Venus POD

Nammu and Malachi were standing by the console on the Holding Station staring out at the churning clouds of noxious gases exploding from the planet. Malachi appeared in human form but Nammu, unusually for him, appeared in priestly robes, his original form on Earth.

They had been discussing the recent events in Maddy's life and her discoveries about the lineage of her family. At the moment they were comparing it with the lineage of Jonah's girlfriend Philippa.

Thoughtfully, Nammu said, "You know this is no chance convergence of circumstances."

"What do you mean? Jonah meeting Philippa?"

"Yes, I think the Ancients are trying to mend rifts."

"I am not sure I understand." Malachi, puzzled, turned towards Nammu.

"You remember our discussions regarding ascending to Source. The Halqu so far have been unresponsive to offers of options to realign; their actions concerning the Alignment have shown they are not interested. In a convoluted way, via Jonah, I think they are offering Philippa's family the chance to connect up and resume a route back to Source."

"Well, isn't that assuming that their lineage is a true one down from the Ramoindine Dynasty and before. It's still not totally clear, is it?"

"Let's put it on hold for the moment as we have visitors," concluded Nammu.

Nammu turned as Simon and Maddy entered the chamber. Simon looked rather uncomfortable having never been to a meeting off Earth.

"I hope you are coping, Simon, I know this step up may be taking a toll on you. Your resonance is not used to this higher frequency. We felt you could manage it and obviously we can help you should you need additional support."

"I am feeling well at the moment, though my physical body is reacting, my heart rate seems to be beating faster and I am feeling light headed."

Nammu went to Simon's side and placed his right hand over Simon's head and his left hand over his heart. Simon immediately sensed a slowing down of his heart rate and felt re-energised.

"Sit down here and you can share our conversations."

Nammu directed him to a floating chair which closed around his body and raised him to be on direct eyeline within the small group.

Nammu turned to them.

"Welcome, you have had quite an eventful time recently. We have been observing so are aware of your concerns."

Maddy looked at Simon whose face said, "I told you so."

"We have been looking at Philippa's lineage and your concerns and instincts regarding her are correct. The connections between your families go right back to the beginning of your Soul contract Maddy, in Sumeria, 8500 years ago. It is from her lineage that betrayed you to the Halqu; originally when you had to be taken to Egypt and more recently in the thirteenth century to incarnate in France."

"You mean Malena and her escape to The Croft?" interposed Maddy.

"Yes, and then to the sixteenth century and, as it was clarified by your grandfather's research, the Ramoindine dynasty dissolved. Philippa de Lomagne d'Anduze, was the woman who finally inherited the lands of the Counts of Toulouse but the lands were then absorbed into the Roman Catholic Church. It left her family very bitter and they were very resentful about losing their lands. It was a relative of theirs at that time who betrayed the identity and location of Malena, the then Sentient Seal, to the Inquisition. This was obviously manipulated by the Halqu who whipped up the crusade against the Cathars as an excuse to track her down. Philippa's family were not active supporters of the Cathars, they veered more towards the Roman Catholic church. However, their resentment about losing their lands was used by the Halqu as a means to manipulate them to support their quest. We think unfortunately they are still being manipulated despite the fact that the Alignment has passed and that they are working with the Halqu. What we are concerned with at the moment is their reasoning, Why?"

Maddy was alarmed.

"What can be their current significance? They lost their purpose with the passing of the Alignment and I thought they had disappeared."

"Well, the portals are still vulnerable even so but we are checking."

Nammu turned towards the console and made a series of hand movements. The console lit up and showed a number of eagles hovering over several locations.

"The sites you can see here are the Shield locations and they look peaceful, there is no activity going on at all."

Turning to one of the screens he made a slight movement with his finger and within moments the eagle on the screen swooped into the Chamber. Settling before them his form changed into that of a being with red skin and long hair parted in the middle drawn into a bunch at the back of his head. Around his neck hung a Collar similar to the one in Maddy's possession, carrying the same symbols.

"Greetings. Are there any developments?"

"None, it's quiet, no movement over the Shield portals and so far no appearance of the Halqu or other visitors physically on any part of the planet. They may of course be hovering outside the dimensional field, observing, but even so we have had no 'electro-magnetic' interference which would imply this."

"Good, your vigilance is still required as we are not confident of their intentions. Return to the sites and anywhere else if you think there is concern. Perhaps you should also go on to the grid around the planet and visit the old centres of civilisation; Stonehenge, Machu Pichu, Angk Wat. Anywhere that was on the same ancient energy grid as the Pyramids. You never know where they might make a base. Go now."

With that the being gradually faded to his bird form and swooped out of the room.

Maddy noted the exchange and remembered the eagles at The Croft and how they appeared at regular intervals. They had been checking and guarding her. Malachi also noted this and remembered Nammu telling him that he had sent extra Marechal.

Nammu turned to the group and spoke deliberately.

"The planet is undergoing many troublesome events, we do need to consider the plight of the population of Earth. We need to find out whether Philippa's family is involved with the Halqu. Perhaps that will give us a clearer idea as to what is going on. We know you have been invited to her family's estate. Are you able to go and use the opportunity to find out?" he asked Maddy and Simon.

They replied, "We have already decided to go."

"Good, I thought you had. Let's part now and meet again after your visit. In the meantime we will try and find out if they have an agenda which might be impacting on the planet's current situation."

Nammu disappeared reciting.

"All time, all things are now and complete."

-◇-

Malachi accompanied Maddy and Simon to the transfiguration booth and they all returned to The Croft. Malachi left them and retired to his house in the village.

Simon and Maddy rang Grace and made plans for their visit to the UK and Lord Andrew's estate.

-◇-

Chapter 15
Vaxchtajn and Lord Andrews

Some days before the events that had transpired with Maddy's family, Lord Andrews had retired to his country seat having put in motion the instructions Vaxchtain had given him regarding the Arks. He was currently perturbed by the news his ex-wife had given him about Philippa and her boyfriend. It was apparent that the relationship had become serious.

His housekeeper Amy came to the door of his study where he had been sitting for some time contemplating events.

"Sir, sorry to bother you but there is a gentleman asking to see you. I took him to the library."

"I wasn't expecting anyone, did he give a name?"

"No, but…" and looking awkward she added, "he does look rather exotic." raising her eyebrows.

"Thanks, I'll go and see him."

Amy disappeared and Lord Andrews made his way to the library. Entering, looking around he couldn't see anyone. Turning to leave the room to ask Amy if she had been mistaken, he halted on hearing a rustling sound. He saw a dark man in full middle eastern robes moving towards him. Lord Andrews saw through the disguise that it was Vaxchtajn who was hovering in the corner of the room.

"It's you Vaxchtajn."

"Yes, I think I rather startled your servant. I was going to summon you but the matter that is manifesting at the moment requires urgent attention. It concerns your daughter."

"Philippa, she's at school. What's happening? She isn't in danger, is she?"

"No, not in danger, but we are going to be found out. She has made friends with a boy and the relationship is developing fast. We foresee that they will marry."

"Hang on, she is only 17 and I have only just been made aware of her having a boyfriend."

"Well, she has and it is getting serious."

Lord Andrews dwelt for a second on the conversation he had had with his wife only the day before.

"You remember the Seal we were searching for at the recent Alignment? Well, the boy's grandmother is that Seal. Due to a death in the family they have uncovered a great deal of information which is leading them to you and us. They are very distant relatives of yours. Back through your previous incarnations you have betrayed them again and again from the beginning of our quest. The family are reincarnated descendants of your adversaries and carry the lineage we sought. They are the true inheritors of the Counts of Toulouse, the Ramoindine Dynasty and therefore any claims you think you might have as descendants are null and void because of them. How far they are into realising the family connection is one thing but the danger is that they will find out about our current project. Having thought they had dealt with us and we were out of their way after the Alignment they will realise we are back. At the moment they think they have rid themselves of us."

Vaxchtajn continued, "There is also the possibility that we are being manipulated at a greater level."

"What do you mean?" asked Lord Andrews.

"It may be that the Ancients are trying to draw us back to Source, the path to enlightenment, using your daughter in order to engineer this."

"You really think so?"

"At the moment we don't know. We need you to get in touch with your daughter and find out about her relationship with this boy. How serious it is? If it is serious, you then need to suggest a meeting with the boy and his family, perhaps a visit to your estate."

Looking around Vaxchtajn added, "They cannot fail to be impressed by your history and the wealth on display. We do know they want to meet you which means they are suspicious."

"How do you know? Are you spying on them?"

"You know as an adept of a high level we do not spy but that we see all things and are aware, but not always of potential outcomes. They appear in many and various forms."

Pausing, Vaxchtajn studied Lord Andrews who was absorbing what he had been told.

Vaxchtajn continued, "So invite them and let's see what happens. In the meantime to safe guard our plans, in case it leads to them intervening, we are going to speed things up a little. Act on what we have discussed and we will meet and let you know the next step."

Lord Andrews turned to ask him what he meant by 'speeding things up' but Vaxchtajn had disappeared.

-◇-

Lord Andrews stood, troubled. The sun shone through the stained glass windows leaving a rainbow of light oscillating in the room adding to the strangeness he was feeling about Vaxchtajn's visit. He also had a deep sense vibrating through his body of the imminence of a catastrophic change that was going to occur to the planet and to the human species. He had had no idea of the existence of Philippa's boyfriend or whether it was serious until he had spoken to his wife. It was his own fault; he had not seen Philippa or his wife for some time.

There was a knock at the door and Amy entered.

"Sorry, m'Lord, there is a phone call for you, it's Lady Philippa."

Distracted he turned.

"Thank you, Amy, can you transfer it? I will take it in here."

"Hello, Philippa, how are you?"

"Fine, Daddy, and you?"

"Oh, so so, I spoke to your mother the other day."

"Oh, perhaps she told you about Jonah."

"Yes, so that's his name."

"Are you coming up to town soon? It would be good to get together and I would like you to meet him."

"Well, I had no plans to do so as I have only just returned after a long trip. I decided to stay here for a while. Is it important that I should meet him?" Lord Andrews asked tentatively.

"Not necessarily, but he has become a special friend. You know that some of us from school go into the local town each weekend; that's where I met him along with a lot of other locals our age. It is just that we have become closer as we share a lot of the same interests. Anyway, I want you to meet him. Mummy thinks you should. She seemed a bit, well, put out for some reason, going on about us going to University and the future, losing touch, you know. He is really nice, you would like him I'm sure."

"Very well but I can't leave the estate at the moment as there are too many things going on. How about you bring him down here for a weekend, perhaps even invite his family? They might like a weekend break, there is plenty to do here. Where do they live?"

"Nearby, in one of the small villages outside the town I visit at the weekends. Okay, I'll ask him and get back to you. Bye…"

Well, let's wait and see what happens now, thought Lord Andrews.

-◇-

The Legend d'Anduze

(From time indeterminate)

The story tells of a Knight, two metres tall with broad powerful shoulders and girth. His hair and beard were white. His hands huge and vice-like gripped the cross-handle of his sword that was scythe sharp. The sword belonged to his father; it was a family tradition where it was handed on to the eldest son of each generation. It glittered and glowed in the blazing midday sun that beat down relentlessly from the cloudless azure sky.

Strong and purposeful he was fighting in the Crusades. He was a ruler of domains in the southern regions of France but at the time was fighting by the side of the King of France in the cause of Christianity.

Reaching Jerusalem, having successfully vanquished the enemy for the moment, he was pausing to rest with the men he commanded. All were weary and hungry and the streets and squares and watering holes surrounding the centre of Jerusalem were full of these fearsome fighters, their tension needing release. No tavern, brothel or for that matter, woman was safe from their rampaging thirst.

Our Knight, the hero of our story, was more than weary. This was his second campaign and he had seen everything, and more, before. He felt older than his age and tired of the travelling and the bloody fighting. 'God' was surely testing him, as cutting and slashing through the enemy lines, a sickness passed over him that asked the question 'was this really what God intended'.

As a Knight and gentlemen of royal lineage he was accommodated in the royal palace in luxurious quarters with all attendant privileges. His great uncle had been the most celebrated leader of the First Crusade and another uncle had declined the crown of Jerusalem.

His mind settled on peace and escaping to Southern France. He woke in the middle of the night to see a figure standing at the end of his bed. To him it was fearsome, tall and wraith like, writhing in spirals of light. Speaking in his mind it told him he had to carry out a mission, that he must return to his homeland, escape the battlefield and await instructions.

His life had purpose and would end in France.

-<>-

Chapter 16
The Weekend Break

On the plane back to London Maddy was amazed that things had moved so quickly. No sooner had she and Simon left Nammu and Malachi and reached the Croft, than the phone had rung. It was Grace who told her about further arrangements and that Jonah was a little taken aback that the invitation was extended to include his family. Lord Andrews had phoned Grace and told her that there were many things for them to do on the estate, including horse riding and swimming in the indoor pool.

As they realised it was soon, they had made travel arrangements and here they were on the plane descending into London Stansted Airport. When they reached Arrivals they saw Jonah waiting for them.

"Hello, darling, we didn't expect you to be here."

"Lord Andrews, Philippa's father has sent a car for you so I thought it would be easier if I met you. It all seems rather elaborate considering he and I have never met," said Jonah, looking slightly perplexed.

Maddy sensed that Jonah was feeling uncomfortable at what he thought was a great deal of fuss over his relationship with Philippa. As they walked towards the parking area Maddy asked, "How close are you to Philippa?"

"It's a bit of a sore point with Dad at the moment. I've applied for the same university as Philippa; we are very close and don't want to lose one another. We have a sort of," and he hesitated, "let's say a commitment. I suppose you would have called it an engagement in your day. I think it's why Dad and Philippa's dad have got our families together this weekend. They think we are too young."

"Our generation sees things very differently from yours. I am not trying to be rude but we have matured much more quickly too."

By this time they had reached a car, *Limousine more like*, thought Maddy giving a side glance at Simon who rolled his eyes. The driver opened the door for them and they set off. The journey took just over an hour and they picked up Grace en route. Richard, Grace's husband and Colin had decided not to accompany them.

After a short time the car approached some very magnificent wrought iron gates, the entrance to the estate, and then they were driven about two miles before the car parked in front of a very well maintained Queen Anne mansion. It was beautifully renovated. *It must cost a fortune to keep up*, Maddy thought as her eyes ran over the facade of the building and around the perfect landscape surrounding it. It was to her taste as it was elegant but simple rather than grand.

Helped out of the car and assembling their luggage they turned as an immaculately dressed man walked down the steps to greet them. Maddy was taken aback, he was so handsome. *Not another one* she thought remembering her first meeting with Nammu. *He was probably in his early sixties*.

His hair was greying at the temples, his face was lightly tanned, and in build he was tall and athletic. His jacket, shirt and trousers, expensively cut for all their casualness, were pristine and imparted a sense of ageless aristocratic bearing and assurance. He moved towards them with his hand outstretched.

"Hello, how good of you all to come. I hope you have had a good journey. You probably will need a rest. Philippa arrived this morning."

At that moment a very beautiful young woman came bounding down the steps and flung herself at Jonah. She was stunning with long blonde hair cascading around her face and down her back, crinkling in exquisite ringlets obviously naturally curly. She was oblivious of the effect she was having. Like her father she was tall and athletic with startlingly blue eyes the colour of violets. Her skin was creamy and clear, her limbs long and finely-toned. Together she and Jonah looked like an advanced species that had just landed on Earth. Maddy was reminded of the unusual colouring of her mother who had told her that her eyes had been described as the colour of lapis lazuli.

Maddy stepped back observing their exuberance and naturalness together as they both helped take the luggage into the house. She realised why Jonah was so smitten with Philippa and remembered feeling the same when she first met Colin at University. She looked towards Lord Andrews and saw him as fascinated as she was at the spectacle of their children's closeness.

Breaking the spell Lord Andrews ushered them all into the entrance hall and called Amy to help take their luggage to their rooms. The hall was vast with what, Maddy thought, must be portraits of their family. The resemblance to members of her own family struck her. There were shields, high on the walls and up the sides of the balustrade in the entrance hall, the floor a rose pink marble. Again she felt the stirring of her memory and she shuddered. She immediately recognised the emblem of the Counts of Toulouse and St Gilles.

Standing by them Lord Andrews noted her interest.

"Welcome to my estate. I see you are fascinated by the shields, you probably recognise them as they are of the same region of France where you are now living, Mrs Jameson. The history of those goes back a very long way, ending around the thirteenth century when my ancestors estates were absorbed into the Church's lands."

He paused and looked around at each of them intently as if gauging their response.

"Anyway, let's get you settled in. I have given you all rooms on the first floor overlooking the gardens. Let's meet in the Library at 6.00 pm and we can have some pre dinner drinks. By the way my name is Raymond but everybody calls me Ray, let's dispense with formalities as our children seem to find those old fashioned these days. By the way my ex wife will be joining us, she is yet to arrive."

"Oh, I didn't know Mummy would be coming," piped up Philippa.

"Yes, it was a late decision on her part, she said she wanted to see you and meet Jonah's family."

Turning to Amy.

"Amy, can you show my guests to their rooms?"

As they followed the housekeeper Lord Andrews said, "See you later" and with that he walked off towards some large heavily carved double doors with detail, which he opened and went through.

Maddy, Grace, and Simon followed Amy upstairs to suites of fabulously furnished rooms.

Amy asked Maddy, "Would you like me to unpack for your Mrs Jameson?"

"Thank you, no, I have only brought a few things."

Quickly emptying her case, Maddy went next door to Grace's room and found Simon with Grace.

"Well, I am speechless, what do you think? Knowing what we do now from Jack's notes the connections to our family are obvious just by looking at all the shields and portraits in the entrance hall."

Simon said, "There seems to be some undercurrent. I am not sure but my gut feeling is that we have been manipulated to come here either by Nammu and the ancients or by the Halqu. It all seems to have happened so quickly. There seems to be some urgency about what is happening."

"I agree, it feels bizarre, everything – the setting, the coincidences. But we suspected that might be the case," added Maddy.

-◇-

After resting and changing they went down to the entrance hall where they were directed to an enormous reception room and then led through to what was obviously the library. It was slightly more cosy with an enormous log fire burning. Crystal glasses glistened on a table to the side and Lord Andrews was pouring out the drinks. It was all very convivial, the conversation light and centred around Philippa and Jonah who were looking slightly uncomfortable and at pains to tell everyone that they saw a shared future together.

They talked of University, both interested in astrophysics. Philippa wanting to be an astrobiologist, Jonah inclined more towards physics and quantum mechanics. It appeared that they had already discussed having a gap year so that they could visit the many ancient heritage sites throughout the world which, they informed everyone, were based on the constellations,

Maddy and the company were entranced with their enthusiasm. Amy entered the room to let them know that dinner was to be served and was followed by a very beautiful mature woman.

Philippa exclaimed, "Mummy" and rushed over and threw her arms around her.

Maddy engrossed in talking to Lord Andrews turned and came face to face with Philippa's mother.

Maddy instantly recognised her as Arabella, the woman whose house Sarah, her friend in France, had taken her to for the workshop and meeting with the Psychic Pam.

Lord Andrews introduced her as Lena who was working the room, shaking everyone's hand. A waft of very expensive perfume assailed their senses.

Lady Andrews was classically beautiful Maddy noted, studying her more closely than she had done in France. Tiny and svelte she shared Philippa's colouring. Her hair was cut in the same severe fashion as Maddy observed in France but more coiffured and shone like sheer silk. Her make up and clothes one could see cost the earth, her shoes delicate and extremely high heeled.

She did not seem to have recognised Maddy at all and Maddy was uncertain as to what to do, whether to acknowledge their previous connection or not.

Breezing over the obvious affect her introduction had had on the group, Lady Andrews suggested they follow Amy and ushered everyone to the dining room. Obviously, thought Maddy she had lived in this house and now acted as if she was the chatelaine of the mansion. Simon commented how well the house had been preserved in its original Queen Anne style.

"That's down to Lena," said Lord Andrews. "When we came here it was in a very poor state and she made it her project. We inherited it from her family who originally came to England from France after the Hugenot's turmoil. Our ancestral heritage is mixed, French and Italian. Mine from the Toulouse connection and Lena's going way back to the Medici."

"My ancestors came from Anduze, north west of what we know as the Carmargue area. We were originally named d'Anduze and it has become anglicised over time to Andrews."

"Medici," said Simon picking up on Lena's connection. "That's an interesting connection."

Lena responded.

"Yes, I have a very distant relationship to Catherine d'Medici. She had several children and my line comes down from her daughter Claude who married the Duke of Lorraine."

Lena continued, "Catherine was a very interesting person notably recorded as a murderess, poisoner. However, if you read about her background you realise she became a very bitter person resulting from her childhood and unfortunate marriage to the Valois, Henri II. He had a lifetime love affair with Diane de Poitiers which was the bane of Catherine's life.

Instead of screaming and shouting at him and leaving him she bore it. When he died it seems that was when she was at her worst, she took the power as Queen Regent and ruled by terrorising her children. Her sons were quite young when they came to the throne, one mad, Charles, but all terrified of her. So…"

Lady Andrews paused and looked around the table into everyone's eyes studying their reaction…

"You see, though one can be appalled at her murderous actions one can see how she arrived at being how she was."

Maddy felt that Lena appeared to be excusing the Medici practices and wondered if it revealed an interesting characteristic of Lena herself.

A quiet descended over the company. Maddy was feeling uncomfortable, she was having flashes of a previous life lived during the reign of Catherine de Medici. She sensed she knew Lena from that incarnation and the feeling she was getting was of absolute dread. That Lena's incarnation had been probably as manipulative as that of her distant relative Catherine. Scenes of dead and bloody bodies filling the streets. Feelings of absolute terror and hiding, then running, alone. The scenes changed to visions of the sea and a boat.

Maddy looked up and saw Lord Andrews staring at her intently.

He asked her how she came to live in France. Maddy explained about Colin's project and that eventually they had divorced. She made her life seem very ordinary, introducing Simon as a cousin she had only recently connected with via her mother.

"I knew that she was French. As a family we never spoke about it, probably because she came to England as the second world war broke out and she was only 18 at the time. Things were very different then."

Maddy turned to Lena. Now everyone had had a considerable amount of drink they were all more relaxed, she felt she could perhaps challenge Lena.

"I think we have met, just once in France. I may be mistaken?" she asked.

Lena's eyes narrowed, a hard look came over her face, and she studied Maddy intently.

"I don't think so, though you do look slightly familiar."

"It was in France, my friend Sarah took me to your house for a meditation workshop, about two year ago."

Lord and Lady Andrews looked from one to the other.

"How interesting. You were in France, then Lena. In fact you were there for some few years, you've only just been able to sell your house and return to London," said Lord Andrews.

"Yes, it took ages, the housing market is not like the UK. Well, I am sorry but I don't remember our meeting."

"Well, as I said, I might be mistaken, anyway the name of the person I met was introduced to me as Arabella." she retorted boldly looking questioningly at Lena.

"But, Mummy, that is one your names," Philippa chimed in.

"She has several Christian names, some of them she has passed on to me," continued Philippa.

"I am Philippa, Madeleine, Catherine. They are old French names, significant in our ancestral history."

"As you say it is all very interesting," murmured Maddy, not quite sure how to deal with the situation. She felt awkward and turned the conversation to Lord Andrews.

"I can see your connections with France and especially to the South. I recognise the cross. Where I live there are many examples of it. So does your family have a background from there?"

Lord Andrews explained, "Their French title was connected to the Counts of Toulouse and inherited from the last Count, actually a Countess Joan. The family who inherited, as I said were from Anduze north of the Carmargue area but eventually gravitated to Paris and then to England. The change of name was brought about because my family then were heavily involved in the Protestant movement and were refugees escaping the persecution, predominantly in Paris. They originally settled in London, Spitalfields and prospered but then moved out and acquired this property which was smaller originally but they then developed it in this style. My office is based in Spitalfield where I also have a small apartment for when I am in London."

Philippa who had been preoccupied talking to Jonah, turned and started talking animatedly about the history of the family.

Philippa explained her ancestry, the baronetcy of Lomargue and Anduze and change of name to Andrews for simplicity and anglicising it; repeating a great deal of what her Father had said. But she also went on to tell of the persecution of the Cathars and of the Counts of Toulouse family, who were sympathisers.

"It seems our family has always been on the run from persecution, mainly because we pursued a protestant cause, first the Cathars who were considered heretics and then the Huguenots."

Lord Andrews looked on amused not realising how interested she was in their family history.

"Yes, and we have a story about our family that has come down from the Crusades, we call it a legend though really it is just a memory about a very famous and courageous member of the Ramoindine dynasty."

Maddy started, the word 'legend' and reference to Ramoindine dynasty was clinching their families tightly together.

Philippa related the legend in an exaggerated romantic tone and ended by saying that her ancestors probably predated the Ramoindine. Philippa said she had thought about the mission the Knight was given frequently but had had no luck finding out what it was. She looked towards her father.

"Can you throw any light on it, Daddy?" While she had been speaking he had been pouring out more wine for everyone but seemed to have withdrawn, as if he was anticipating her saying something that he did not want everyone to hear.

"No, I can't help you, Philippa, it is a bit of a mystery, but then it is just a story."

Having studied everyone including Lord Andrews while Philippa had been speaking Maddy wondered what it was he was hiding. She looked at Simon who seemed to have shrunk into his chair. The atmosphere was charged with things not being said. Her mind drifted momentarily into a trance like state and…

I visualised a scene from a previous incarnation and recognised Lena though not as she was currently. A courtesan in elaborate gown, decollage revealing her breasts, her face heavily painted and hair elaborately dressed being followed by a huge party of revellers, drinking, bawdy. I felt myself shrinking into the shadows of a recess in what must be a castle...they passed...

She came to and glanced around and found Lena studying her intently. Simon broke the atmosphere by saying.

"You have an extensive library, Lord Andrews, have you any books relating to the history of your family?"

"Yes, I think there are a few, perhaps tomorrow we could look at them, it would be interesting. I don't have much time to do that sort of thing so it would be entertaining."

By this time an uncomfortable silence had descended on the dinner table. Philippa had finished talking and dinner was over so she jumped up and asked her father if she could show Jonah around the house as he was interested in the architecture. The parents thought probably that it was more about having an excuse to be alone together. Lord Andrews nodded consent to the couple and turned to Maddy.

"Tell me, Maddy, are you settled now in France or do you intend returning to the UK? Your husband lives here but you say you are divorced?"

"Well, it is a bit of a story actually with which I won't bore you further other than to say that though I wasn't keen initially I have grown to enjoy living there. Whether we keep the French house or not, not sure, but for the time being I consider it home."

"What about the culture and language? How are you getting on? Do you speak French now? It is a region of France steeped in a rich history especially the middle ages. Do you know much about it?"

For some reason Maddy felt a chill pass over her, as if to warn her to be careful of what she was saying She felt he was probing to see what she knew or understood.

Lightly she offered.

"Yes, of course, you couldn't live there without knowing eventually about the Cathars. It's still felt very deeply in that area. I joined a history group and it was evident amongst the members that there still is some bad feeling between the Roman Catholic Church and, let's say, sympathisers of the Cathar faith. It still lingers on. Can it not? It was one of the greatest European genocides, it was the reason the Inquisition was created for and which then swept Europe."

"Well, that is interesting," Lord Andrew replied. "And do you have any personal allegiances to the history?"

"Afraid I haven't. I had a very eclectic religious upbringing which left me with a very open mind about the concept of God. In fact you could call me a pantheist actually, I am very interested in the Earth and growing things. I have a large garden in France that I love."

Changing the subject she asked, "You have many acres here on the estate as well as diverse occupations. Is this your main one?"

"Most of my time is taken up with managing the estate though I am by profession, with a University degree, an astrophysicist. I studied at MIT in the States. It is my only other interest but the estate has made me side-line it. My interest focussed on the evolution of the Planet, that is Earth and its position in the universe."

Maddy found his eyes penetrating her and her colour rising. She realised that he was reading her mind and he was being helped. She could feel it. She also felt something happening to herself as well, of a sudden she felt her past coming to her, not only her present incarnation but she could feel her mind scrolling back through time to the beginning. She must not let him in and she put up a mental shield. Surprising her self that she could do this but realised her waking up was rolling faster and faster and she had certain powers. She quickly moved adjusting her position and glanced around the room sensing another presence. Looking at Simon who had been listening and observing she saw him flinch.

Calmly, turning directly to Lord Andrews she said, "Is it of concern, the evolution of the planet?"

"Well, the way we as a species have used it, I would say yes," Lord Andrews replied vehemently.

"We are 9.2 billion in population and overloading the capacity that the planet's resources can sustain and behaving badly. The population needs waking up. As a species and that is what we are, we seem to think we have control but one can see the more we think this, the more things are getting out of control." Lord Andrews was heating up to his subject, pacing urgently around the room.

"Waking up, what do you mean?" asked Maddy, side glancing at Simon for support.

"A shock, recent catastrophes have proved that in those circumstances the species rise above their indifferences, compassion appears and they work together."

"Isn't that a rather drastic view of things and resolution to the problem? You surely can't be saying that more catastrophes would be a good thing?"

"Well, once the shock has been absorbed by the viewing majority, let's face it, looking at the news reporting these shocking events, depending on where you are, it's viewed almost like looking at the latest blockbuster movie. No, it needs a global catastrophe involving everyone to wake them up."

Lady Andrews who had been sitting very quietly through these exchanges interrupted with, "I think it has been quite an intense evening for us all. Shall we call it a night? We have plenty of time tomorrow."

On this note Maddy sensed Lady Andrews had interceded as she could see Lord Andrews was getting more and more agitated. Maddy wondered if she was in on what she now had come to the conclusion was some plot or project going on behind the scenes.

"This has been such an interesting evening but it has left me very tired and it has been a long day," concluded Maddy.

"Of course, can I get Amy to send something up to your room, a tisane or other drink?"

"Thank you, no, and thank you again for having us here. I'll say good night." Maddy left for her bedroom. The others all said their good nights and went to their rooms also.

-◇-

Simon and Maddy left Grace, Jonah and Philippa with Lord Andrews and made their way upstairs. Entering Maddy's bedroom they decided to discuss the evening.

Maddy jumped in first.

"That woman is lying, she is Arabella, she must have integrated herself into the community in France along with George Bottomley looking for me."

"What do you think?" asked Maddy.

"Something's not right. I think all our suspicions were correct. He is definitely mixed up in something and so is Lady Andrews," replied Simon.

"Bearing in mind Nammu asked us to arrange this visit and the way it just happened," Maddy said.

"It definitely has to do with the Alignment and the aftermath. I think the ancestors, Nammu on our side and the Halqu with Lord Andrews have engineered this. I had a trance after dinner and it was of an incarnation in which Lady Andrews was there. There is something malevolent about her. I don't trust her. I think she is involved. Though they are divorced it doesn't mean they don't have an understanding which involves the Halqu. However, I think Philippa is totally innocent, just as Jonah is, of their and our goings on. Hence why she was sent away to boarding school. It would be good to get closer to her and try to draw her out about her childhood as I think something must have happened. You don't send your only daughter away to boarding school. A son yes, but not a girl."

"I agree. It is all too coincidental. I don't think we can find out anything more here, do you? Let's try and leave tomorrow. We can meet Jonah and Philippa and question her away from here."

-◇-

Chapter 17
Maddy Reflects and has an Encounter

After Simon left her room Maddy felt restless and took a long bath to try and relax. Enjoying the luxury of the elaborate furnishings and tray of drinks left for her she fell back on the bed into a deep sleep.

Dreaming…it was paradise, I am strolling, floating over verdant pastures by a running stream. The stream was gushing through the rough stones, frothing and throwing up a mist carrying leaves and twigs like tiny barques full of spirits. I sensed a presence and turned, a huge lizard rested before me, it had numerous arms moving in a wild frenzy, its jaws snapping. Fearsome as it looked, I did not flinch, but stood my ground…

Maddy was woken suddenly by a noise she couldn't identify; putting on a dressing gown she furtively crept out of her room and along the landing. She came to a balustrade which opened out over the grand reception hall. Carefully she peered over the banister and looking down saw a giant reptilian creature in the hall below. With limbs flailing it was communicating with Lord Andrews in a strange guttural language. Memory flooded back to her, she had just dreamt the incarnation which was back in Egypt. It was a species she had encountered before, a long way back. It was malevolent and she could see that it was having a dramatic effect on Lord Andrews who was cowering beneath the animated dialogue. So, that was who the Halqu really were.

-◇-

Having returned to her room after what she had witnessed she decided to take up Simon's suggestion about leaving as soon as they could. Feigning the onset of flu symptoms, Simon and Maddy left the others to enjoy the rest of the weekend and returned to Colin's apartment to work out what they should do. Maddy remembered Michael telling her about love and how this can combat threat and fear, though now, she did not feel frightened due to her recollecting her soul's journey. On the journey back she focussed on sending out unconditional love frequencies for protection.

First of all, with Simon's agreement, they felt they should report to Nammu and Malachi.

-◇-

Likewise, accepting gracefully the departure of Simon and Maddy, Lord and Lady Andrews stood on the top step of the entrance hall and waved goodbye. Turning they looked at each other.

"As Vaxchtajn said, things have to move on quickly now." Lord Andrews muttered. "They have worked out everything and that is why they are leaving early, the look on Maddy's face said it all. Maddy is the Seal the Halqu have been searching for and her family are now suspicious of our plans. We must tell Vaxchtajn."

"What do we do about Philippa?" asked Lady Andrews.

"We can't leave her here. We put her through so much therapy and then sent her away to school. We are going to have to let her in on all this."

Lord Andrews. "Yes, we will have to. I agree it is not going to be easy, I think she may be difficult. Let's get everything in place to leave and then decide how to handle her. Let's go back to London and get organised. I'll get in touch with Vaxchtajn," finished Lord Andrews.

They parted and Lord Andrews made his way to his study and sent a message to Vaxchtajn confirming their next meeting and suggesting they speed things up for departure. Vaxchtajn replied that the Arks were ready to leave.

What to do about Philippa? Lord Andrews thoughts then began to weave a scheme as to how to get her to accompany him.

-◇-

Chapter 18
Nammu and Malachi Ponder

On the POD orbiting Venus, Nammu and Malachi had been watching the events of the weekend. They also saw Vaxchtajn appear on the night that Maddy witnessed interaction between him and Lord Andrews.

"Well, our doubts are confirmed. They are the link which has betrayed the *Sentient Shield*. It is obvious that Lord Andrews is the Halqu's puppet and probably an ancient. This is serious as the Halqu are now aware of Maddy's role and of Jonah's involvement with Philippa. I am also wondering whether at the original setting up of the Shield Philippa could also have been a Seal."

"They haven't told Jonah of any of this or the past events have they?" asked Malachi.

"No, so we have time. But we need to know what the Halqu are up to."

"We need to follow them, I am surprised the Eagles haven't come up with their whereabouts."

Nammu summoned the Eagles and informed them of developments and told them to sweep the planet for anything untoward.

"Whatever it is, is well hidden, perhaps with frequency shields."

"Obviously if they have managed to keep underground for so long."

"Perhaps that is it, it is all being carried out underground. Let's do a scan of the planet while we are waiting for the Eagles to return and report."

-◇-

The Eagles sent out squadrons to scan the planet. In their search they came across many archaeological sites of interest. One aroused their curiosity in a remote region of Turkey, six miles from Urfa, an ancient city called Göbekli Tepe. Some locals claimed Urfa was the birthplace of Biblical characters Abraham and Job. There was a great deal of activity judging by the number of archaelogists excavating the site.

As the squadron circled closer they noted rings of huge pillars, towering 16 feet, some elaborately carved with foxes, lions, scorpions and vultures, twisting and crawling on the pillars broad sides.

Another site they came across was the Pyramids of Melnik, a well-known site in Bulgaria without much activity occurring. They were natural, sand pyramids formed because of the soil erosion. The height of the sand formations was up to 100 metres and constantly changing in the course of time, similar to those found in the Tet valley in France, and used in the Alignment.

The Eagles continued to swoop and soar as if searching for prey. Eventually something caught their attention and the squadrons converged on a site in the very North of Scotland, in Great Britain.

What they saw was activity involving huge land clearing vehicles covering a vast area. Their attention was particularly drawn to a runway which was approximately 3 miles in length. One of the squadron, having swooped very low over the site had also picked up an entrance which was large enough for the huge vehicles to pass through. They saw massive earthmoving vehicles coming and going. On several turns their many eyes clicking open and shut several times they took reconnaissance photographs which they immediately transmitted to Nammu on the POD. With their task finished they left and returned to report.

-◇-

"Well done," Nammu remarked on the Eagles return and turning to the console brought up the photographs.

"What's going on there?" asked Malachi as he viewed the activity on the screen.

Nammu quietly replied, "It looks as though they are building runways, an airport or a spaceport more likely. Look at the activity going in and out of this entrance here."

Nammu pointed to the side of the aerial view. Malachi got closer to the screen and discerned huge earth moving vehicles, lorries and jeeps driving along the roads leading to the entrance.

"I see what you mean, it is all disappearing into this entrance."

"As I said, I think the Halqu are using frequency screens to shield from satellite surveillance, otherwise we would be able to pick up more about what is going on underground."

Pointing again at the screen Nammu said, "There, at the activity, and further down, there are convoys of trucks coming up to that point."

"Yes, obviously what is being prepared for is imminent. We need to view what is going on in space. I have the feeling that the runway is going to be used for a shuttle to take people to a space ship, probably waiting somewhere in outer space."

Looking at the console, at space out beyond earth, the moon and the nearer planets, Nammu could not see anything amiss.

"They must be using a cloaking device. Their technology is very advanced, I need to call in the ancients to get past it. I need time to do so and I can find out about Philippa at the same time. Whatever they are doing, based on what Lord Andrews said about the plight of the planet, there must be a catastrophe about to take place. Let's look at the tectonic plates and see what's going on."

The console revealed volcanic activity on the Pacific rim and by the look of what they could see, warnings were going off on all the sites set up to record activity.

"I think the Halqu are triggering some major earthquakes which will mean tsunamis; this will be a worldwide extinction event, we must act, fast. We need to check on Lord Andrews and where he is going."

-◇-

Chapter 19
Ring of Fire and Sleeping Giants

Nammu invoked an audience with the Ancient Guardians. Subsequently he was summoned to Alcyon in the Pleiades. It was an ethereal setting, its luminosity so intense that Nammu felt himself absorbed into the eternal being where differentiation between space and time do not exist.

By telepathy he relayed his suspicions to the Guardians, of whom several were present. They confirmed his thoughts regarding the redirecting of the Halqu's goals back to source. They noted as he had, that so far there had been no effect regarding this. The Halqu were still on a one track mission.

Hence the reason the ancient Guardians had drawn Philippa and Jonah together. Both children had been seeded, their mitochondrial DNA had been kept pure from way back through the aegis of time by the ancients to keep the lineage on track. They were seeded to be symbiotic with the planet's mineral, gas and base elements. That was why the goal was for Maddy to be ultimately used for the Alignment.

The Guardians also relayed a sombre picture of the likely outcome of the current events, saying that the Earth was going to be swept clean by the Halqu so that they could return and take over the planet. They also said that there were obviously other outcomes as the Earth was also evolving in several different dimensions and time/space existences whereby all was not lost. As they said, nothing ever is in the Universe, it is just a question of the universe constantly evolving and healing itself. It is only the species on the planets who hold their own destiny, their survival in their own hands.

The question was which species would survive? Which specie deserved to survive? What was important was the harmonious evolution of the universe. It was not a question of the ancients going in to rescue 'deserving' species, it was for the species to work it out for themselves.

However, the ancients did emphasise strongly, if the occasion arose whereby a species, or event was likely to disrupt the eternal core harmonic of the universe, then they would take action.

They portrayed to Nammu the many dimensions that earth might be evolving in. Therefore, the current events were only one pathway out of countless ways the earth could go.

They gave the example of current events on Earth regarding climate change, how it was speeding up and the devastation globally due to the warming of earth. Snow caps were melting, methane bubbling under the permafrost in the Arctic could cause a major fire hazard to the planet, sea levels rising, flooding. Currently the human race was well on the way to wiping itself out.

The ancients pointed out one of the most dangerous situations regarding a possible extinction event.

The ring of fire around the Pacific rim has always been under threat of volcanic eruption and earthquakes. They referred to these as sleeping giants.

They pointed out that the scientists on Earth, with their recent developments in technology and photography had enabled specialists to be able to map the floor of the ocean. What it had revealed had been a shock. Many volcanos were active underwater and on the verge of erupting. In the specialists' view these eruptions/earthquakes could happen at any time, now or in years to come. Should they erupt, research had shown the effect it could have on the Pacific. Huge Tsunamis would result, in wiping out all the rim countries on the Pacific. They also referred to the corresponding plate activity in central America, Yellowstone Park with the same prediction, estimated likewise to erupt at any time and similarly in Central Europe, notably Italy.

Immersed in this knowledge Nammu knew that the Halqu would be fully versed with this and from Vaxchjtain's threats knew this was what they were going to do; trigger activity on the plates. He also knew that it would be nothing to them as they had all the necessary advanced technology to make it happen without suspicion falling on them. Earth's populations would also accept that it was all due to climate change and it would not occur to them that there was any extra-terrestrial interference that had triggered the extinction event.

-◇-

Chapter 20
Philippa Panics

Lord Andrews, though not totally sure what events were forthcoming knew that it meant he had to escape with his family and quickly. According to what he understood from Vaxchjtain the planet and its inhabitants were about to be wiped out. Vaxchtajn was offering him the chance to escape and he was going to take it.

He was now frantically packing and making arrangements to leave after a heated exchange with Vaxchtajn who had finished by telling him, "There is no time to lose now, they know our plans, we have to leave now. I am going to trigger the plates."

Closing the house and making arrangements with the staff who ran the estate while apparently conducting himself as if nothing was amiss had taken its toll. Sadly, he realised that his staff would perish in the forthcoming events. Packing his car with his personal needs he drove fast to Philippa's school making his way directly to the Principal's office.

"What a pleasant surprise, Lord Andrews. Philippa will be delighted to see you."

"I wish this was a social visit, Principal. However, unfortunately, Lena, my wife, has had a serious accident and I need to take Philippa to see her."

"Oh, dear, I am sorry, I will send for her straight away."

The Principal went to the outer office and told her secretary to fetch Philippa.

Philippa arrived saying.

"Daddy, what a surprise."

"Darling, Mummy has had an accident and it is serious. We must go to her. Go and pack your things. We had better hurry."

Philippa now looking distraught rushed off and returned with her bag.

Walking out to her father's car she tried to find out what had happened.

"Where is she?"

"In London, that is where we are heading."

Both were quiet in the car until they reached London.

"Which hospital is she in, Daddy?"

"One near the town house."

"I didn't realise there was a hospital near there."

"Well, let's just get there, shall we?"

Philippa sank into silence but then realised that they were going to the town house.

"Are we going there first?"

"Yes."

Lord Andrews now resolved to be as monosyllabic as he could get away with.

Philippa puzzled, realising that her father was not saying much, thought it was because he was concerned about her mother.

Entering the house she was greeted by her mother who rushed towards her.

"Mummy, what's going on? Dad said you had had an accident."

Her father followed and closed the door and confronted her.

"We need to leave London as quickly as possible so go to your bedroom and pack as much as you can into the cases Mummy has put there for you."

"This is bizarre, what do you mean leaving and packing everything? What's happened and why did you lie to me about the accident?"

Lord Andrews explained that they were going to Scotland to a space port, from which they would be leaving to go into space.

"You are joking, aren't you? This is wild going into space, why?"

Her father looked to Lena, who nodded at him.

"You must tell her the whole story despite the consequences."

Her father explained to Philippa the history of the contact with the extra-terrestrials, in particular with Vaxchtajn.

"You mean what I saw when I was little actually were monsters, real!" Phiippa exclaimed.

"You sent me to a psychologist for years trying to get me to believe it was my imagination. And you now say that they are telling us that we have to leave the planet because there is going to be some disaster that is going to threaten the population of the whole world? Well, I don't believe you. I am not going. I think you are both mad."

With that Philippa ran upstairs and locked herself in her bedroom.

Lord and Lady Andrews decided they needed a plan of action.

"What do we do? I am not leaving her," Lena said remonstrating with her husband.

"Well," Lord Andrews said. "We could sedate her."

Raising his eyebrows questioningly.

"That's drastic, and she would catch on, it would be too suspicious."

"But it may be the only way…we need to see what her reaction is…give her a bit of time."

"Have you any sedative?" Lady Andrews asked.

"No, but I have someone who owes me a favour, a doctor, he lives nearby."

"Well, get it and then we can think about other options at the same time."

Lord Andrews picked up the phone and made the call.

"He says I can go and pick it up now, so I will do that."

"Try and get something we can slip into a drink…not an injection."

"Okay, in the meantime try to calm things down. Explain a bit more to her and the consequences of staying on the planet."

Lord Andrews made his way to the front door. Lena followed and mounted the stairs to Philippa's bedroom.

-◇-

Philippa, shocked at the story her parents had told her about what was going to happen, phoned Jonah to tell him what had been said.

"What do you mean you are leaving the planet? Look, calm down, tell me what they told you."

"They told me about some extra-terrestrials that they have been communicating with, well, ages probably before I was born. They have lied to me and manipulated me…telling me things were all in my imagination when I was a child…sending me to a Psychologist. It's awful. They are absolute liars."

Her voice trailed off, she was crying and frightened.

"I feel they are kidnapping me. I feel as if I don't know who they are any more."

"So what are they planning?"

"We are supposed to be going to Scotland to some space port and then going into space…I don't know any more."

"Well, calm down and try and find out more, leaving the planet seems crazy unless they are saying the planet itself is in danger of destruction."

"That's it, that is what they are saying and the consequences of staying are dying, not just me but everybody."

"As I said, try and find out more and in the meantime I will talk to Mum and Dad and get back to you."

Taking in what Philippa had told him; *and Grandma who had been acting a bit strange recently,* Jonah thought to himself.

Jonah had taken the call on his mobile phone in his bedroom where he had been studying. Rushing downstairs he was greeted by Grace. Frantic he explained to her his phone call with Philippa. Grace called Maddy who was with Simon on her way to see them.

-◇-

Leaving Nammu and Malachi Maddy was returning with Simon when she received the phone call from Grace. When they arrived at Grace's they found Jonah pacing up and down frantically talking to his mother.

"What's up?" asked Maddy, concerned.

"It seems Philippa's parents have been acting very strangely and…have kidnapped her."

"Kidnapped her, that is a bit dramatic, isn't it?"

"No, it's true, they took her from school, lied to her about her mother having had an accident and when they arrived in London Lena was there, nothing wrong with her. They said they had to leave immediately and told her to pack her things. I said I would talk to you but she has texted me since and told me that they have left. What can we do?"

Simon, Maddy and Grace exchange looks, Grace looked accusingly at Simon and Maddy.

"Simon, I think we need to do some explaining."

"Yes."

"Jonah, sit down. Grace, make us a drink. We have to tell you what has been going on over the past few years. It may seem strange but please hear us out."

Sitting down Jonah, said, "Well, hurry up. I think we have to track them down and the more we wait the farther they have gone."

Maddy and Simon explained the Alignment to Jonah, and Maddy's incarnations and Simon's role, the visits of Malachi and Nammu and the threat of the Halqu. Jonah took it all in apparently unfazed, and Maddy wondered whether it was because his generation's desensitisation through the media.

She further explained the current situation created by the Halqu and the plight of the planet.

Jonah's reaction, amazing to Simon and Maddy was of accepting it all.

"At the recent weekend break we discovered Lord Andrews is mixed up in this. As I reincarnated so have Philippa's parents, they have all been involved in the Alignment struggle."

Jonah interjected, "Philippa mentioned her parents had involved her with a Psychologist when she was young, implying that it was all in her imagination but she now realises it was all true what she saw."

Maddy continued, "The current situation is that the Halqu are instigating a major planet extinction event in which most of the population will die. The Andrew's purpose for taking Philippa is to get all three of them off the planet, this has obviously been planned."

"She said they had mentioned Scotland, a spaceport."

"Yes, we think we have located it and that there are space shuttles waiting to take off. They are taking the privileged people, those that have paid for a seat."

"So what do we do? Are we leaving too?" Asked Jonah.

"Yes," answered Maddy.

"You are telling me everything is being planned, you were going to expect me to go with you without question?"

"No, we were going to explain everything to you. We have already explained to your mother but recent events overtook us."

"I am not leaving without Philippa, we have to go and get her."

Simon volunteered.

"Maddy, take Grace and Richard to Nammu and wait for us there. You can all prepare to leave. I will stay with Jonah and go and get Philippa. We can head north and stay overnight at my chalet in the Lake District. Get on to Malachi, Maddy, and get him to track Lord Andrews down and the exact coordinates for the space port. Okay, Jonah, go and get a bag with a few overnight things. Let's go."

Watching Simon and Jonah drive off, Maddy turned to Grace and Richard who had just arrived.

Hesitantly she said, "I have some more explaining to do before anything further is set into action."

-◇-

Chapter 21
Maddy Explains to Grace

Grace and Richard looked expectantly at Maddy who began…

"I know that I have explained to you that I am an ancient guardian – you still might be having trouble wondering what that really means."

She looked from one to the other.

"Grace, you met Nammu, he appeared with the cat, Isolde, who is a Marechal, a guardian, though not at the level of Nammu or myself. I explained about Malachi, that is Michael, is also a Marechal."

"I need to explain to you my use of the word level. It's not level in the sense of good or bad or higher or lower; it is a process all beings go through to arrive eventually at Source, a state of 'all knowing' or 'eternal existence'. We are all at different stages in that process – life throws you challenges that enable you to pass through into the next stage. Each stage gives enhancement, powers that are used for positive use. What is happening at the moment is 'forcing' us all into leaping forward quicker than perhaps we, or you, need to at the stage you are currently going through. How we all cope with that is an individual experience."

"We have to leave the planet and you will be subjected to experiences that you will have difficulty understanding. It is necessary to leave as the Halqu, the bad group who have been following me through time, are triggering an extinction event on the planet. You, like myself, have had many reincarnations, on the whole not remembered but you probably will have experienced 'deja vu' from time to time that may have left you a little puzzled. All of the people you are meeting at the moment have been there with you throughout your incarnations, all for reasons necessary for your soul process – you are there for them for the same reason."

"I have also to explain to you about dimensions. Earth exists with you in a dimensional field tied to three dimensions. Our experience, every aspect is tied to that dimension as you are to the planet. However, there are other dimensions running in parallel which cannot co-exist with each other but they are there. Scientists on Earth are aware of this but so far cannot access these. However as an ancient, I have powers to travel dimensionally, and back and forth in time. There are other species who are able to do this.

"The reason I am telling you is because early in my present incarnation, here on earth, from when I was 11 to 34 years old. I had debilitating health problems and it was only the intervention of the ancient guardians that saved my life. That period of time was influenced by the Halqu who were abducting me for genetic experiments. The abduction process damaged the reproductive organs in my body. Aware of all this, and because it stood in the way of my achieving my goal, the Alignment, at that time the guardians moved, let's say, that Maddy into another dimension. In this dimension you only know me as your mother."

"The Maddy in the other dimension continued her life and lurched from one trauma to another. Her goal, in conversation with the ancient guardians, was that she didn't want to come back physically and therefore would do anything to achieve eventual spiritual commune with the universe, that is, not reincarnate. That Maddy is still on that course.

"I have diversified, to continue. The ancient guardians' intervention resulted in saving a child born to that Maddy, due to the special nature of that Maddy's mitochondrial DNA and its evolutionary strength. The ancients saved the child and removed it to a special holding base on a healing planet in the cluster of the Pleiades in the constellation of Taurus."[11]

"In my present incarnation, in dreams that I call white dreams, my counterpart dimensional self and I have visited the child since her birth to the present day. Her name is Magda, and Grace, she is your counter dimensional sister."

"I am telling you this now as when we relocate to our new planet she will be there. Due to her upbringing she is now an ancient with associated powers and she will be there to meet and help us."

Maddy finished at this point studying the effect it was having on Grace, who looked stunned.

Grace uttered quietly.

"This is just adding more to what I have already had to take in, what we have all had to adjust to. One of the things I am having difficulty with is that I feel I don't know you. I have glimpses of my mother as I knew her but it has changed. I am not confused any more. I realise we are all in grave danger and we just have to go along with whatever is about to happen."

Maddy added, "It's a good point when we are relocated on the other planet there will be support to help everyone adjust. This all has had a long history and everybody we know and have contact with has been there all along through time…so there will be many memories that will crop up and need to be dealt with, as there have also been many historical betrayals."

Maddy had been as concise as she could but then stressed the need to assemble those who were going to leave the planet and explain to them why this had to happen. She turned to Grace and Richard and said, "Right, we need to go! But first, Grace, I must take you to meet Magda."

-◇-

Chapter 22
Evacuation

Maddy decided it was time to take Grace to meet her other dimensional sister. She realised it would be a test for Grace who had not experienced anything other than a three dimensional earth experience. Linking telepathically with Grace, Maddy stepped up through the frequencies, and took her to the POD orbiting Venus.

Gratifyingly, Grace seemed to make the transition effortlessly, which led Maddy to believe that she had indeed inherited her genetic disposition and was probably an ancient, or high level Marechal. Grace, however, was still oblivious of the theoretical implications of what was happening, which thought Maddy, was not a bad thing; she was acting and responding emotionally and intuitively which was more important.

Grace and Maddy were greeted by Malachi, Isolde and Nammu. Magda had also been summoned and Grace, having been told about her sister, eyed her with interest.

Nammu welcomed them. For Grace's benefit he had assumed the costume in which he had appeared at the Croft when she had first encountered him.

"The Alignment has passed and we are now awaiting the outcome; is the planet going to ascend to 5D or remain in 3D and continue with its struggles, is the question? Unfortunately, in the meantime, we have discovered that the Halqu are planning an imminent planetary event which could mean the extinction of the human species. We have to consider getting some of you off the planet."

Grace interjected, "You seem to be addressing this situation to me so I am assuming you all…" She paused and glanced around at them, "along with my mother are not human, and that you have powers and technology whereby this event would not affect you."

Nammu responded, "Putting it bluntly, yes – however, you and your heritage, plus more of the human species have the potential to have the same powers. That is why the Alignment was so important. It would mean the human species would ascend to a higher level of universal existence; released from the hologram you have been trapped in for thousands of Earth years."

"We must deal with the evacuation of a number of you to ensure the purity of the human DNA can be preserved. It is valuable to the future of universal harmony. Many species in the universe have benefited from the inclusion of DNA human mitochondria in their individual species concoction as have the inhabitants of the planet we are going to. Its main contribution to genetic engineering is that it allows genetic biologists to elucidate evolutionary relationships among species."

"What we are talking about here, though, is gathering a group of humans and taking them off earth. Do you know what kind of extinction event the Halqu are planning?" asked Maddy.

"We are not sure but we think it likely they will manipulate the tectonic plates to cause major eruptions, volcanos and earthquakes. Where the centre point of this will be we can't be sure. We are looking at the plates on the Pacific Rim and Yellowstone Park in the USA. These have always been a threat, they could erupt tomorrow or in hundreds of years' time. The Earth's mantle has become increasingly fragile. It is always moving, and eruptions will always occur, but the Halqu could cause this to happen any time."

"You mean a planet extinction event would happen anyway it is just a question of timing?" Grace ventured to say.

"Yes, it happens to all planets, from time to time in their history. It is the evolution of the universe, a fact, natural."

Malachi included himself in the conversation.

"Earth has had the additional problems. The predominant use of fossil fuels and over population have contributed to the acceleration of the planet's warming and is causing drastic climate change. Additionally, development of the atom bomb and more recently the development of particle colliders in the USA and Switzerland have begun to cause dimensional disturbances which could contribute to the unbalancing of the planet. Tapping into the nature of reality there is the danger of accessing other dimensions. Without full knowledge of Universal Physics, Earth could become fragmented and hold back the development of this harmonic universe of which it is part and it would send out further unbalancing ripples throughout the Universe. At this point it could also destroy the planet's electromagnetic field and it would become like the moon without any gravitational shield, it would be like a barren and empty vessel."

Nammu took up the conversation again, "The Halqu and those Earthlings supporting them, the Sharrapuk, are playing with fire. The ancient Guardians have from time to time, during these human scientists' experiments, intervened to prevent catastrophic disruption to the planet."

"Along with this the planet Nibiru is returning. Its orbital path seriously affects the Earth when it passes and could cause an extinction event as it has before. The last great flood on earth was caused by its path. The Annunaki, Niburians, evacuated and watched this. They returned and rebuilt what was the beginning of your civilisation. Initially they put their species in charge and initiated wise earthlings whom they had trained to take charge. However due to fighting between two Niburian brothers, they created a war and another extinction event occurred. However, at that point the Annunaki, left and allowed you the survivors of that civilisation to develop."

"However, as you most probably can deduce it led to the development of the various hierarchical religious nonsense that has led to all your wars and still continues."

Maddy could see that Nammu was becoming frustrated with what he had witnessed on Earth through millenia of Earth years and that Earth had not moved on – it was stuck with the general level of education and ignorance of the populace and their amnesia regarding their connection to the planet they had been left to care for. Nammu had turned away in sorrow and frustration. Gathering himself he turned back.

"So, we have to get you off the planet to enable your species to survive, give you another chance to prove that you can rise above petty differences and attune to the Universe.

We need to gather as many of you as possible who understand the predicament. We need to get you to safety and then assess the situation for your future.

So what do you think about the people being rehoused on another planet?" finished Nammu.

Maddy as an ancient, like Nammu, looked towards Grace as representing the human species.

Grace asked, "Is it a possibility to move to another planet and how would we get there? I can understand that there are other planets out there, probably capable of atmospheres that compare favourably to Earth; but they must be light years away."

"Yes, you are right. We have been assessing several planets. There is a planet called Essassani. It is approximately 500 light years from Earth near the Orion constellation, 300 to 700 years into the future on a separate time line. It is no longer in Earth's frequency band and therefore undetectable by your scientists. The inhabitants of the planet live in a future period equivalent to Earth's twenty-third century on the same time line. It is a little smaller than Earth."

"We have approached them and they are very willing to set up a housing station unit to orbit their planet for Earth's population independently and are eager to assist."

"They derive their energy from a pyramidal power source fed by the universe, the same system that the pyramids were constructed for on Earth millennia ago. It is a natural source of energy very different from what you know."

Grace asked, "But how do we get there? It seems to me that it will require a massive effort gathering people, and the number of space ships required would be immense, hard to imagine. I mean just gathering everybody would be a major problem."

"Unfortunately we would not be taking the whole population and we won't be going by the same method as the Halqu. The Halqu with Sharrapuk plan to leave the planet physically in spaceships, which is a laborious way of doing things; living on spaceships for many years while searching for other habitable planets. This has been planned by the Halqu as they really don't want them to survive, they are deceiving the Sharrapuk."

"So you mean they have intentionally misled Lord Andrews and the Sharrapuk?"

"Yes, they will wander in space and the Halqu will return and take over the planet. The Sharrapuk will never return unless as slaves to the Halqu. They will either die in deep space or perhaps find another planet eventually and be abandoned."

"Would there still be this Earth as it is, and could we return to our lives as they are now?" Grace asked.

"That is a pertinent question and I am sorry to say that probably not. The planet in this dimension after an event like this would need to settle. Species like the Annunaki are able to come and go, periods of time, let's say thousands of earth years can pass, and they could come and go, monitoring when the planet would be suitable for habitation. To them, it would seem like a blink of the eye. Their time recording is different, as it is on all other planets. Planets relate to the sun they are orbiting and the length of orbit."

"Yes, Earth would be struggling, probably for millennia."

"However, if it ascends, that is if we succeeded at the Alignment, then that overrules all that is happening at the moment. You have to understand that several versions of earth exist in different dimensions, all with potential probabilities and outcomes."

"But unfortunately, from our recent information about the Halqu and their plans it is not going to happen on this earth in this dimension as it is suffering too much and needs to be swept clean."

"So what is the point of our surviving?"

"The point is, your soul will survive and your mitochondria DNA which is a necessary part of the evolution of the universe and all species within it. It is important for genetic engineering of 'ascension genetics'; species evolving in harmony with the harmonic universes and back to Source. Simply put 'love' – positive energy, light is the source. In fact, the Essassani DNA is part made up of the human species."

"How would Earth be?"

"Should you return to Earth it would be in symbiosis with the planet and seed the evolutionary process. The plan was that Earth, would develop to be a recreational paradise with a library of DNA of all the species in the universe."

"We cannot predict how Earth would be; nothing is fixed and several potential futures are occurring concurrently."

"It could be a recreational paradise such as Essassani or it could be robotic, driven by technology, machines. Human beings could become robotic, their cellular structure and brain linked to central computers for management of the species."

"Your soul will come back, if you choose it to, to help re evolve Earth.

Another frightening reality is that there are other species who might visit and harvest humans as food. The spark that is soul within humans acts like an energy charging battery; as humans take food and vitamins pills, it acts in the same way for them. We could be their food and vitamin pills.

There are further horrifying pictures we could paint of future scenarios for earth – we have seen these in other parts of your galaxy and further out in the Universe.

You have to understand that your species has been an evolving one. You are not an original species or race, you are a mixture of DNA that has been refined from DNA source banks throughout the universe and even your present DNA has been used to hybridise other races of extra-terrestrial beings.

If the Halqu return with the Sharrapuk as their slave race there is no knowing what they would do. In the past the Annunaki, of which the Halqu are a relative, mined the planet and tampered with the genetics of the indigenous earth species to produce a slave race to manipulate and work for them. The majority of today's population are descendents from them. The Annunaki created the base religions so that they could maintain their control to date. That is what ascension, the Alignment, was all about, escaping from their tyranny which has been a question of mind control over thousands of years.

However, the human species are becoming aware of the fact that their inherent DNA contains the 'God' factor which overrules the Halqu's manipulation. Due to the Alignment, they, too, are aware that the planet is waking up and are threatened.

It seems to me they probably have given up on returning to their original home and have focussed on Earth, and by manipulation intend to return after the extinction event and take over the planet."

Malachi interrupted, "Perhaps we should get on with the plans regarding evacuation."

"Where are we with the situation about raising frequency?" asked Nammu.

"It's going well, it is evident that the younger generations are aware to an extent of the global situation and becoming active. They seem to be more spiritual than previous generations and concerned about climate change. The ancients have interceded and sent emissaries to seed these generations. They are however a highly technologically aware generation, and the media feeds them every kind of fantasy through movies and computer games. This is a control and conspiracy ploy of the negative forces."

"They are all able to access the internet however poor their families may be. They are able to deal with fantasy and fact and make reasonable assessments of the comparisons. It seems to have given them a new mindset to be able to deal with 'let's say' reality?"

"BUT there is one problem with the easy availability of mobile phones, ipads and such like. They are obsessed by them and their connection to the physical reality of the earth has become distant. They prefer to be, it seems, in a virtual reality world."

"Convenience and access to everything is easier than 'doing'. The population explosion has also meant that people are living in cities, in multi storied blocks of living accommodation, which has removed them from the basic survival factors for example, not lighting fires for cooking and warmth."

"The film industry and media have been unhelpful and controlled by the Elite. They have desensitised the population with violence in films, reportage. The majority of the population live in fear. Should the earth's population be reduced to basic existence without energy supply they would have no skills to help them survive."

"And what is worse, they are affected by space fiction films which depict hostile reactions to extra-terrestrial visitors. Believe me, any extra-terrestrials visiting Earth have travelled many light years with highly developed technology. Does the average human brain not have the rationality to realise that they don't stand a chance against them? Human beings and their hostile reactions show an arrogance about their place in the universal order."

Nammu, aware Malachi was getting rather heated on the subject interceded, "Well, there is that aspect of dimensional reality and the future, it can go many different ways."

"Does choice enter into this?" asked Grace.

"Yes to a point, but of course there is the majority opinion; what is available easily sways development in different directions."

Impatient Malachi pushed the urgency of the situation.

"So, what do we do, how do we gather those who are going to the new planet?"

"First we must gather those who will be leaving with us. Get in touch with the light workers and alert the ascended. Maddy can head this up and we must all meet and go through the aspects of travelling by light. When we meet, we will give more information about the planet and how we will be travelling. You have to go and decide how you are going to explain all of this and who will be accompanying you to the new planet. This is a matter of urgency, you have only a few days to gather everyone and explain. We will be living as guests on another planet until we can return to Earth but they must understand that time/space probabilities will mean that when they return Earth will have moved on, probably thousands of years into the future and what state it will be in by then is indeterminate."

Nammu concluded with, "Now go! All time, all things are now and complete."

-◇-

Chapter 23
Reconnecting with Pam
and the Lightworkers

Maddy and Grace stepped back to Earth, Maddy returned to the Croft in France and Grace to her home in the UK. Both were in a state of high energy realising the enormity of the task before them, gathering as many of the highly spiritual population they could. Both realised the difficulty they might have with immediate family; Maddy's brother Charlie and then her sons Mark and David. Maddy thought they probably would not accompany them as she had already experienced their scepticism.

-◇-

Grace was pondering on the location of Simon and Jonah, whether they had actually managed to find Philippa. She picked up the phone and Jonah replied.

"Where are you now?" she asked.

"We are at Simon's chalet in the Lake District. Someone called Michael turned up and told us that Philippa is en route to a space station in the very North of Scotland and that we are not far behind her. I didn't know such a station existed," he added wearily.

"So what are you going to do?"

"First light tomorrow we are going North and try to intercede before she reaches the station. With a bit of luck we should get her tomorrow."

"Be careful!" Grace exclaimed, "you can't be sure how violent they may be."

Jonah asked, "How are things with you?"

"Can you put me on to Simon, Jonah, I need to talk to him."

"Simon, Mum and I met Nammu yesterday and we have been told we are going to leave the planet. Very soon in fact. It seems urgent. We have to gather as many people as possible."

Simon hesitated, there was a slight pause before he responded, "I thought it would come to that. So what is the plan?"

"Well, Mum and I are trying to co-ordinate a gathering of light workers and others who would be able to ascend. Nammu and Mum are organising a gathering as well as locating a point from where we will be leaving. How we are going to travel I have no idea, not by space shuttle. We were told Nammu would explain this. A bit mysterious, but that's all I can tell you for now."

"Well, we will do what we can to find Philippa and get back to you as soon as possible."

Putting the phone down he turned to Jonah and told him to get a good night's sleep and be ready to leave early the next morning.

-◇-

Sitting on the terrace of the Croft Maddy was deliberating on the visit to the POD. With the threat of the extermination event imminent she realised she had to make decisions quickly. Her thoughts moved to thinking about Jonah and his retrieving Philippa. Lord Andrews and Lena, colluding with the Halqu were determined to take their daughter with them on the evacuation in spaceships. She wondered how much Lord Andrews was aware of the Halqu's plans. Nammu suspected they were being deceived as the Halqu wanted to return to an Earth purged of the human species and to use it as their own planet. If any Earthlings, as Maddy herself was now calling the human species, made it back with the Halqu then she feared they would be used as slaves, much as the Annunaki had genetically engineered previously.

Putting that aside she focussed on Nammu's plans, that her current incarnated family and extended population of light workers would leave Earth to survive. He had further explained that the Halqu's method to remove the Sharrapuk was rather antiquated, that he would be using another method; travelling a different way was how he had described it to herself and Grace on the POD.

As an ancient she knew he was referring to the crossing point of light, understanding of which was going to be difficult to explain to those they would be taking with them, including Grace. However she felt they could engender their trust.

She was now thinking back as to who to take and who would help her gather them. There was no question, it had to be Pam, the light worker, who had helped her during the Alignment. Picking up the phone she made the call…

"Pam, sorry not to have been in touch but I need to share something with you and it is urgent."

Maddy told Pam the conversations she had had with Nammu and what was about to happen.

"So," said Pam. "I can see we need to gather people. There are many who are ascended light workers acting as mentors to groups all over the world. I have been one of the co-ordinators of this work, and we have been telling them of the Alignment and what happened. We have succeeded in helping many to ascend to the appropriate frequency."

"That's promising. I need you to send out word of what is happening. You may be met with some scepticism, but for those who understand you must tell them that we will be gathering to leave the planet. The venue for the gathering has not yet been decided but when I find out I will let you know. It will be in the next 24 hours."

"You must tell everybody that they can't take anything with them. It will be difficult to make them understand this, but you probably can envisage that things can be re-manifested where we are going."

Pam replied wryly, "That may be difficult, you know how acquisitive even enlightened human beings can be."

"Well, let's hope we can get the point over. Let's leave it like that for the moment, see what you can do. We need to move quickly."

Pam replied, "Let me know as soon as you can where we are gathering as obviously some will have a long way to come."

"I will, it will probably be in France."

With that they ended the call.

Pam sat with the telephone in her hand gazing out onto the garden she had tenderly nurtured, all the herbs and flowers which were now flourishing. She mused over her encounters with Maddy and the journey they had shared leading to the Alignment. With sadness she realised that she now would be leaving this all behind, for what and where she questioned.

Maddy had not been specific, but as a light worker she knew her spiritual journey was setting off again on another destiny which she had to follow.

-◇-

Chapter 24
Nammu and the Meeting Place

Maddy decided she had to reconvene with Nammu as soon as possible to find out about the meeting place for departure, and also about the planet they would be going to. Having regained her ancient powers she stepped up through the frequencies and directed herself to the POD. Nammu greeted her, as did Malachi and Isolde.

"Welcome, Maddy, events are moving rapidly I see you have activated the light workers. We are sensing a rapid rise of frequency from all over the planet."

"Yes, I need you to tell me the meeting place and also about the Planet we are going to. I can't remember ever having been there," she said reading his mind.

"No, your incarnations and soul ascendancy have not encountered that constellation before. It has become a seeding centre for this harmonic universe. DNA seeding has been distributed from there."

"Essassani is a planet that operates in the 4th/5th level, therefore a higher frequency than Earth and accordingly has different characteristics which you need to know about. Their time line is 700 years into the future of Earth, but within the same dimensional field, so not skipping into another dimension. They share a parallel reality within the same dimension."[12]

"Its inhabitants have a DNA mix of ancient Pleidian, Annunaki and Human beings, earthlings. They communicate telepathically, but can speak, their language is the ancient one but because they are a mix which includes earth they can understand many languages. They have communication devices which they use when meeting people so it gives them the language they need to communicate."

"With the help of the ancients and Pleiadeans and other aliens they are learning to be half physical and half spirit. That is why we have chosen this planet as by ascending it is the direction Earth is going to."

"The planet's frequency is a much higher rate than Earths – it fluctuates between physical and non-physical reality and its current population is hybrid as there is a hybridisation programme linked to ascension. In other words attaining 5th dimension the last of physicality and beginning of the return to light – to source."

"The Planet itself has a different chemical mix, more oxygen, giving their species a red tinge to their skin. The surface of the planet is left to evolve naturally and used as a place of leisure. The population live in ships orbiting the planet and that is convenient for us as they are creating a ship for your population to live on. You will obviously have interaction with them and be able to access the surface of the planet for leisure as they do. It will be like going on holiday, taking a break."

"They are organising a reception committee for your arrival and an orbital unit where you will live. It will be like a laboratory initially as there will be a necessary change to your body make up that I will also explain. It is to do with how one travels from one planet to another in the space/time continuum."

Nammu paused and Maddy asked, "It all sounds very good. You say there is a reception committee. What can we expect?"

"The orbiting unit you will inhabit has been specially created, it is new and comprises their latest technology. In the meantime, however, what you have to impart to your people is for them to understand about travelling by light and dematerialisation and re-manifestation."

Maddy nodded sagely.

"I see that I have a lot to explain. Should I use the visualisation of the Merkaba; obviously we will be using DNA crafts that have the Merkaba as part of their craft dynamic so I can lead into that?"

She looked questioningly at Nammu.

"Yes, a good idea, it gives an understanding of anti-gravity."

Maddy asked, "What about the meeting place."

"Yes, we have found a place in France, it is an ancient site, it was known as the Isle of Goats."[13]

Maddy ended the conversation.

"Then I must return to Earth now and tell Pam and the others where we are meeting."

-◇-

Chapter 25
The Gathering

The advance group, Maddy, Pam, Malachi, Isolde and Grace, were seated in a small grotto just outside the cairn on Gavrinis, the Isle of Goats. They were waiting for Nammu. A gathering of lightworkers and associates were massing around the cairn, settling in groups. Richard and Colin were amongst this crowd. Simon, Jonah and Philippa were yet to arrive.

It had been remarkable the way the group had gathered so quickly, as if they all knew their destiny was involved and they had been waiting for this day. Some had knowledge of what they were about to experience. Pam had done her best to send out as much information as she could in a way that would motivate those 'of the light'.

"Where are Simon and Jonah?" Maddy asked Malachi.

"We have lost contact with them but we know they are on their way and not far off. They found Philippa, just in time. They managed to locate her at the space shuttle station just as she was boarding. It was a tussle with her parents. Anyway, they let her go."

Their attention was diverted as Nammu appeared with Magda by his side, both robed as ancients.

"We have to go as soon as possible. The Halqu space shuttles are leaving as I speak. They are going to a mother ship which is waiting on the edge of the Milky Way, at the entrance to the Rift."

"It was cloaked to hide it but our sources were able to penetrate the shield, so we know exactly where it is and will be able to track it. Our task now is to inform the gathering of their journey and future."

Turning to Pam he asked, "Are they able to understand what is ahead?"

"Yes, we have vetted everybody and are sure they are fully aware."

"Good, then come, let us go and explain."

Rising he led the group to a slight elevation in the ground which was in the centre of the crowd. He began, "You have all been informed of the situation and the planet we are going to."

The crowd nodded and murmured in assent.

"So let us deal with things, first travelling. We will be travelling by light. What we call the crossing point of light, not in space ships. It depends on frequency, that is why we could only be accompanied by those who are able to raise their frequency, their vibration, to a specific level. All here are capable of achieving that frequency."

Someone in the crowd asked Nammu to expand on this.

"You have all been told of Maddy's role at the Alignment and of how she ascended to what we called the Grid for the Alignment?"

"Yes," Everyone concurred.

"A more familiar term for you all might be the astral plain which I am sure you have heard of."

A murmur of understanding resonated around the gathering.

"Some of you intuitives and visionaries are able to access it. Some by using the visualisation of the Merkaba."

Here Nammu turned to the side and with the wand he was holding drew the outline of the Merkaba.

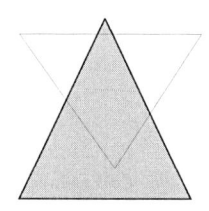

"You can all use this as a visualisation technique to help you. Our travel is similar, the crossing point of light. We have craft that are made of DNA as in the way every particle of our bodies contain DNA. The craft DNA structure and every component particle contain the same DNA. DNA holds memory and can be modified. For example, you, the human species, earthlings, your DNA is specific to you and to this planet. A craft DNA can be modified to incorporate your DNA."

"Like your DNA, which creates and modifies you to your environment, the craft DNA has the same possibilities. Therefore, as one, that is you and the craft, can be programmed by the combined DNA."

"So how does it get programmed and how does our DNA get combined with its DNA?" questions started to come from the audience.

"Because it is out of space/time linear existence, it just is. Together it can be coordinated to go anywhere."

"But surely there must be maps, coordinates programmed in?"

"It doesn't work like that, you are thinking three dimensionally and that which is limited to this planet."

Magda interrupted and looked towards Nammu willing him to calm down.

"This may be difficult for you all to understand. We are taught universal physics in school from an early age."

Grace looked towards Magda and asked, "Where were you brought up?"

"A different planet but one within the star system that we are now going to."

Nammu continued, "On the astral plain you are outside, in a space that is pure consciousness, which you become part of while travelling. You know everything, see everything, feel everything all at the same time. So a different kind of navigating occurs. Hence why Maddy was called the ~Sentient Seal ~ sentience. You become consciousness, feeling all. It is a question of 'placing' oneself in the space time matrix, rather than travelling."

Grace, "I can just about grasp this, how is everyone else."

Nammu cut in.

"You have all been tied to this limited three dimensional experience for your incarnations, but you are actually ancestors yourselves and when you become more 'awake' you will understand."

Grace ignored his interjection.

"But how do we get onto the Astral plain? We are going to have to learn quickly if we are leaving the day after tomorrow."

"Well, I have to explain to you the dynamics of travelling this way and it involves something called the 'Jacket'. Magda is conversant with this and it is probably better that she explains."

Magda moved forward looking around the group.

"Travelling by the crossing point of light involves a transformation of your molecular structure, fundamentally using your DNA to step up your frequency in order to place yourself in space. For ease of explanation I will compare it with putting on a coat or as we have called the process donning the 'jacket'. How do you make this transformation I can hear you ask? Primarily by meditation and self-hypnosis. You access deep into your DNA, very much as the Shaman in your planets evolution have done when seeking answers to questions. It is a question of asking the right questions. To describe the process as producing a shield is not quite correct but helps clarity. The DNA in your body is conducted, instructed by thought and electricity, energy firing throughout the body's neurological and physiological structure. Meditation raises your frequency to a higher vibration; the more ethereal your physical body becomes the more it becomes manoeuvrable in space/time. However it will reach a point when your physical body will actually disappear. You are then able to direct your astral body to the point of destination."

"What must be clear however is that your physical body is connected to this planet. Your physical bodies are made up of the carbon, mineral, gases that make up the wave form frequency of this planet and with which you are in symbiosis. The ancient Egyptians who inhabited this planet would meditate and raise vibration to this level and disappear, however leaving behind their physical bodies in the form of the mummies archaeologists have found in sarcophagi; the residue of the DNA that connected them to the physicality of Earth. This means that should they choose to return they would be able to use the DNA to re-manifest bodies that would be able to interact with the Earth, in other words live at the 3D level."

"This will happen to you when we leave the planet. You must leave remnants of your physical DNA structure so that should you return you will be able to re-manifest here should you wish. I understand that Pam has explained this to you and you have left residue at various locations which are recorded in the Universal DNA library."

"When Nammu described the laboratory unit on Essassini, it is a unit that will help you to manifest a physical body that will enable you to function on their planet. It will be constituted from the 'clay' of their planet."

Someone shouted.

"But how do we do this, time is short to learn all this?"

"It isn't a question of learning. We will go to a platform in the centre of the cairn. In ancient times here on this planet it has been used in this way before. It is a portal to the outer reaches of the universe. I will guide you through meditation and hypnosis. You will be aware but not feel anything other than when you wake, come to, and you will be on Essassani."

"Before we start however, you will be given a small sachet of powder to digest. It is important that you do so. It is a substance called monoatomic gold. It will assist you to attain a higher frequency more rapidly."

Nammu then concluded the meeting by describing in depth the constituent elements of Essassani.

By the time he finished the Gathering had become silent, there was a sense of them comforting each other but acceptance as to what was ahead of them in the coming days.

Nammu left the Gathering with Malachi, Maddy and Magda. He told them to settle everybody and assemble them in groups in readiness for the transition.

-◇-

Chapter 26
Departure

The day of departure arrived. Pam and Grace assembled the groups near to the entrance to the Cairn before sunrise. It was essential that everybody passed through the cairn whilst the sun shone directly along the long upward sloping passage which was orientated to the mid-winter sunrise.

Nammu and Malachi along with Maddy and Magda were in the central room of the Cairn raising the frequency to receive the groups. Time was of the essence as they all had to pass through the cairn while it received the direct mid winter sun.

The central room was designed to capture the sun rays on the shortest day of the year, the Winter Solstice.

Once a year, at the Winter Solstice, the rising sun shines directly along the long passage, illuminating the inner chamber and revealing the spiral carvings inside on the front wall of the chamber. The spiral carvings worked with the mantras chanted by the ancients raising the frequency to the required level. The illumination lasted for only a matter of approximately 17–20 minutes so the groups had been made aware of the need to pass through as quickly as possible.

Walking into the room they would immediately transfer to Essassani.

Seeing the last group disappear Nammu, Malachi, Maddy and Magda disappeared transferring to Essassini.

- ◇ -

Chapter 27
Arrival on Essassani

Dreaming – Maddy was waking up to the memories buried deep in her body. She felt them in every cell, she had no words to describe it, it was a feeling.

These memories did not have a coherent time line, as in past present future, and some of them did not seem to be about her life but somebody else, as if she was living theirs as well as her own.

One moment *she was looking down at her feet, and saw them bare, below a rough wool brown skirt. Looking up she saw a castle tower, looming above her. In her knowing of that moment she knew she was a common serving girl working the sculleries and that the castle was in the village nearby.*

In the next moment she was pondering that there was no history of a castle in the village, but the vividness of the vision made her certain that there had been some such building there in the very distant past.

In the next moment *it switched she was standing in the garden of the Croft, staring up at the sky, deep blue, crystal, the humidity glittering. The smells of September with the slight chill of autumn, advancing, on the breeze. The earth* *was damp and covered with large bronze leaves falling from the mulbery trees and the weeds easy to pull from the boxes in the physic garden. Walking around the sides on the pebble paths, the plants one could gently touch and loosen the soil without disturbing the roots too much, allowing them to breathe.*

Maddy's remembrances were all coming into one single consciousness she was experiencing. She was now here on Essassani. Fully aware now of her soul consciousness and merging with the universal consciousness she realised that she was ethereal and invisible to the others in the room. She saw her family all beginning to wake up, confused and muddled. She also saw the changes in their body makeup. It was going to be difficult for them to grasp these.

Magda was with Grace, so Maddy moved across to her and manifested beside them. Magda glanced at Maddy, who was hovering in a light body, recognisable but ethereal.

Grace opened her eyes and saw her mother and Magda beside her. She looked down, her body was ethereal, hovering. Magda told her not to panic and administered her a potion from a glass vial and passed her hands slowly over Grace's body. Her body started to materialise, watching it she became aware that her body was different, though her mind was still that of her Earth body.

She glanced down and saw her skin had a red tinge.

"What's happened to me? My body feels strange and it is so hot and humid. Where are we?"

"We are on Essassani now and your soul has manifested a body that is symbiotic with this planet. Essassani has a slightly different constituent make up to Earth that is why you are a different colour. There are other changes too."

"Get me a mirror, I would like to see," said Grace.

Maddy and Magda exchanged looks and Maddy fetched a mirror.

"Ah, what has happened." She saw somebody in the mirror she did not recognise. She looked around and saw the others having the same reaction. Her skin was red and her stature smaller. Her hair was white and her eyes were a peculiar shape, almond like with small eyelids and no eye lashes or brows. Her ears were an odd shape too as was her mouth which was smaller with thinner lips, her nose small and snub.

"You will get used to your new look," said Magda. "You have to as it is the only way you will survive here. If you return to Earth you will re-manifest in an Earth form."

The rest of the replaced population were now awake and expressing the same sentiments as Grace. Gathering they looked to Magda for an explanation.

"I told you when you left that there would be changes. I have just told Grace, if you return to Earth you will re manifest in an Earth form. This is this planets 'look' or manifestation and it is constituted on the chemical and gaseous atmosphere of the planet just as your form on Earth is constituted symbiotic to Earth."

A murmur of understanding permeated the gathering, looking at Magda for the further explanation.

At that moment a group of beings entered the room, all with the same body form and colour as the Earthlings had re manifested.

"I am now going to introduce you to the leader of this unit who is going to help you to habituate yourself with your new surroundings. You will all be given living quarters and a tour of the facilities and access to the planet just as if you were inhabitants. You have nothing to fear. This is a most peaceful planet and all the help you need will be given."

At this point one of the beings approached Magda and in language the refugees did not recognise, but seemed vaguely familiar, started talking to her. It was obviously about the procedure.

Observing the exchange Grace was fascinated as the being's lips moved only slightly and the sounds coming from them seemed more like singing than talking. Grace asked her mother.

Maddy replied, "They use frequency rather than hard speech, although speech is a frequency. This speech is more natural and easy on the body as their whole bodies communicate not just their vocal chords as Earthlings do."

"Is that what we are, Earthlings, is that how they refer to us?" asked Grace.

"Yes…just as they are Essassini to us."

"So we are now part Essassani."

"For the moment yes."

- ◇ -

Chapter 28
The Halqu

Vaxchtjain and Lord Andrews were standing by the console on the shuttle leading the convoy away from Earth. Satisfied that the last shuttle had left the planet's atomosphere Vaxchtain turned to Lord Andrews.

"Did you manage to find your daughter?"

"Yes we brought her with us most of the way but the boyfriend and his uncle caught up with us. They were very persistent and put up a hard fight. Time was pressing, your fleet was about to leave and so Lena and I decided that we would leave Philippa hoping that the *Sentient Shield* would protect her. I am not sure what they are doing, I am hoping they are leaving the planet too?"

He addressed this last comment to Vaxchtain requesting a response.

"Well, my sources tell me that they are leaving the planet but at the moment we are not sure how or where they are. They have cloaked their activities but we will penetrate their shield and find out, as their intent, I am sure, is to trace you. We know that from ancient guardians sympathetic to our cause. However our fleet is now approaching the docking station of our mother ship. You need to pay attention and start directing our passengers, the Shuruppak…...."

Vaxchtain chanted, murmuring to himself aside.

NISE MATATI KISITTI QATIYA – People of the land which I conquered, and then PETA BABKA MA LURUBA ANAKU – Open the gate for me so that I can enter here…

and then to the console.

"…to their quarters and give them some introduction to the processes they will be going through and the life they will be living on the station for some, probably long time. It is assimilated to earth time though we are now in completely different space/time measurement."

Lord Andrews paused before moving off the console platform.

"What are our chances of finding a suitable planet to live on until Earth settles?"

"There are an infinite number, the only criterion to concern yourself with is how to survive until we reach one. It may not be their generation that will eventually reach it, or return to Earth. That may be difficult for your people to understand."

"Your technology is highly advanced, won't it over ride the issues you have just related? What about time travel and interdimensional locking. I thought that would override those kind of issues."

"We will explain to you. But for now look at what is happening to the 3D Earth you are leaving."

Turning back to the console Lord Andrews is devastated as he sees Earth being swept with giant tsuanmis, fire and areas of violent earth quakes and volcanos.

"The Earth is cleansing itself and will start again."

Lord Andrews turned again sadly wondering what had happened to Philippa. He had found it hard to let her go and was aghast at her attitude. She had not been troubled at all, she did not seem to care about him.

Vaxchtain watched as Lord Andrews left, and wondered how long before he would work it out.

Vaxchtain saw all. Their journey ahead, aimlessly wandering on purpose and then eventually going to Earth and taking it over renewed and refreshed with the Earthlings as slaves.

He was also aware that the ancient guardians would be watching and trying to interfere.

Let's see he thought to himself who will win.

-◇-

Chapter 29
Finally, Now, Waiting

"So, there now we have it."

Nammu said with his back towards Malachi, Isolde and Maddy.

They were standing on a platform looking down into the viscous churning of the void portal, the Rift. They were tracking the Halqu.

Images appeared and they were looking at a vast fleet of spaceships, silently moving through deep space.

"It will be interesting to count the number of generations that pass by the time they arrive."

"More interesting will be to see how their beliefs, culture, social structures will have evolved, trapped on the ships," remarked Maddy.

"Where is Grace now?" Malachi asked Maddy.

"On Essassani, I have just left her there with the rest. They are in good hands with the Essassani. All a bit horrified at the change in their bodies, however."

"And with her?"

"Those that were on the path of light, or still learning, as she is."

Nammu…

"The planet has been swept clean or that is the 3D version and will restart again with help from the ancients. Earth is now evolving as was originally intended. The Halqu, however, are still weaving their negative loom."

"What will happen?"

"The rules of the universe are always a balancing act; good thoughts create good frequencies that emanate into the universe. The same with negative thoughts. It's not a question of winning or losing. Whether the species created from the original source eventually understands this division – whether there always has to be this battle going on for species to return to source, where there is no division…it just 'is'.

To reach this is the journey.

As humans you can only describe this in terms such as God the creator but in universal terms it doesn't have words or description.

It is a 'knowing' is the closest way of describing it….an existence of forces is the closest I can give you; it is an understanding in symbolic term. Sentience, feeling, the tingle that goes through you when you know something is 'right'.

-◇-

Appendix I
Preface to *The Sentient Shield*
Helen Frindle (2018)

The storyline through this book concerns a journey towards an event called the Alignment; a specific time in the evolution of Earth's history where Earth plays a pivotal part in the overall process of evolution of the Universe. At the point of Alignment Earth, and the Universe of which it is part, is enabled to ascend to a higher dimension, that is from a three-dimensional existence, 3D, through 4D to 5D, ascension being a higher level of spiritual and emotional development. A great deal depends on Earth, and importantly, the spiritual awareness of its population at that time, as to whether ascension can be achieved.

Maddy, the central character represents that which is present in us all and symbolic of the awakening of spiritual consciousness.

This is a fiction in which I have brought together some threads of highly speculative sources, most of which have been challenged by the scientific community since the 1950s.

I must also point out that I am not an historian, archaeologist, physicist or expert in the multifarious scientific professions that may be referred to in this book. I repeat it is a work of fiction. However, I have given some references below in order to clarify some of the terms used to describe events and states of existence in order to give the reader the opportunity to pursue suppositions for his or her own interest should he/she feel moved to do so.

Visitors from Outer Space

Since the 1950s according to the writing of certain authors such as Erich Von Daniken and Zecharia Sitchin Earth has been visited by extra-terrestrial beings whose technological capabilities are far beyond even those we have today.

These visitors may have been responsible for the construction of monuments such as the Pyramids in Egypt, monolithic structures such as Stonehenge and inexplicable phenomena such as those which can only be viewed from the air, that of the Nazca Plains in Peru. For example, the thirty seven mile long by one mile wide Nazca Plain is criss-crossed by geometrically arranged lines according to astronomical plans writes Erich Von Daniken and he questions what purpose would they serve other than as a landing guide for aircraft.

"Classical archaeology does not admit that the pre-Inca people could have had a perfect surveying technique. And the theory that aircraft could have existed in antiquity is sheer humbug to them."

The Anunnaki and the Planet Nibiru

Zecharia Sitchin was versed in Hebrew, Semitic and European Languages, the Bible, history and archaeology of the Near East and was also able to read and understand Sumerian. He wrote many books based on his translations of the cunieform images that can be found on ancient monuments. Many of them depict what could be interpreted as a plan of our solar system indicating nine planets. He proposed an explanation for our human origins that involves ancient astronauts.

"…(he) attributed the creation of the ancient Sumerian culture to the Anunnaki which he stated was a race of extraterrestrials from a planet beyond Neptune called Nibiru. He believed this hypothetical planet of Nibiru to be in an elongated, elliptical orbit in the Earth's own Solar System, asserting that Sumerian mythology reflects this."

Although he sold millions of copies of his books worldwide his ideas have been rejected by scientists and academics…

"…(his) ideas have been rejected by…who dismiss his work as pseudoscience and pseudohistory. His work had been criticised for flawed methodology and mistranslations of ancient texts as well as for incorrect astronomical and scientific claims."

However recent discoveries are now beginning to tie in with his theories.

"…researchers have found evidence suggesting there may be a 'Planet X' deep in the Solar System. This hypothetical Neptune-sized planet orbits our sun in a highly elongated orbit far beyond Pluto. The object, which the researchers have nicknamed 'Planet Nine', could have a mass about 10 times that of Earth and orbit about 20 times farther from the sun on average than Neptune. It may take between 10,000 and 20,000 Earth years to make one full orbit around the sun."

"The possibility of a new planet is certainly an exciting one for me as a planetary scientist and for all of us," said Jim Green, director of NASA's Planetary Science Division. "This is not, however, the detection or discovery of a new planet. It's too early to say with certainty there's a so-called Planet X. What we're seeing is an early prediction based on modelling from limited observations. It's the start of a process that could lead to an exciting result."

According to Zitchin's translations of the Sumerian cuneiform texts which date back to approximately 6000 years Nibiru takes 3600 years to complete one orbital journey. It can be imagined that the gravitational effects caused by the size of this planet could create huge problems for the orbits of other planets when it moves closer to the inner solar system. Recent speculation suggests that this planet is moving towards the inner solar system and will approach the vicinity of Earth relatively soon.

Zitchin further relates that about 450,000 years ago a deposed ruler of the Anunnaki on Nibiru found refuge on Earth. Discovering that the Earth had an abundance of gold he and his followers began to mine for it. They needed gold to repair Nibiru's deteriorating atmosphere.

Due to the difficulties the Anunnaki experienced working in the Earth's atmosphere they decided to genetically engineer the indigenous population of Earth, combining its DNA with their own, thus creating a race of beings to do the mining for them. This genetically engineered race was homo sapiens, us. Zitchin correlates this with the stories of the first books of the Bible and other histories of ancient cultures.

To speculate, if in the foreseeable future the existence of another planet is confirmed might this give rise to a complete review of our planets origins and the evolution of ourselves; the rewriting of our history books and the basis of religions?

Pleiadians

That the Anunnaki may not have been the only extra-terrestrial visitors to Earth and contributed to the creation of our species is also addressed in other literature, raising questions as to the inheritance of our DNA and the possibility that the Anunnaki may also be descendants of other visitors.

The Pleiadians it is alleged were our ancestors; they came to Earth after exploring star systems searching for planets which they could colonise; their own planet, Lyra, was dying. They colonised Earth for a time and have come and gone throughout our planet's history.

Others colonised the Pleiadians, which is located in the constellation of Taurus. Alcyon is the central star of the Pleiades and our solar system along with others orbits Alcyon on a wider orbit.

The technology possessed by the Pleiadians has made it possible for them to travel anywhere in our universe. They share many similarities with us but are more emotionally and spiritually evolved.

Photon Belt

In 1961 a photon belt encircling the Pleiades was discovered. Our sun orbits the Pleiades once every 25,860 years and reaches the midpoint of the belt every 12,500 years and takes approximately 2000 years to cross it. This particular cycle is nestled within a number of greater cycles. In 1962 we entered the sphere of influence of this photon belt.

The energy of the photon belt that Earth is passing through is of a spiritual nature not physical. The 10,500 years of darkness between the 2000-year periods of light afford opportunities for human spiritual evolution.

Precession of the Equinoxes

One orbit of the earth takes 365 days (366 leap year) which gives us one year and our seasons. The earth itself rotates which gives us 24 hours, one day.

- The Earth's axis rotates (precesses) just as a spinning top does. The period of precession is about 26,000 years.
- Therefore, the North Celestial Pole will not always be pointing towards the same star field.
- Precession is caused by the gravitational pull of the Sun and the Moon on the Earth.

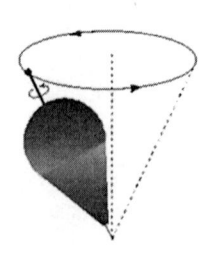

Hence for example references in non-scientific literature to the coming of the 'Age of Aquarius'. Current precession indicates that the Earth is moving from the constellation of Pisces to the view of the constellation of Aquarius. This gradual movement into the new processional cycle is said to have begun around the millennium.

In this book I have speculated that completion of the processional cycle and moving into a new cycle; entry into the Photon belt, and the approach of Nibiru are all happening at this time; hence why I have referred to it all as the Alignment.

Quantum mechanics (also known as quantum physics or theory)

…is a branch of physics; a theory of nature at subatomic level. Classical physics deals with atoms that can be perceived physically. So at quantum level, sub atomic, the physical is divided into particle and waves and can be described as energies. The precise measurement of these energies is expressed by **probabilities** of position and viewed as unpredictable as to eventual outcome. Thus the nature of reality comes into question and suppositions that there are multiple dimensions; that there might be multiple versions of the earth and of ourselves, evolving in differing potential probabilities.

It could also be suggested that quantum theory can be applied to explain many biological and physical phenomena that may be related to bodily function but cannot be proven.

The Nature of the Physical Body (DNA and Cellular Structure)

If existence is fundamentally not physical but a matter of particle and waves, energies, we as beings consisting of billions of particles are subject to the subtleties of the energies and frequencies in which we exist.

According to Russian researchers western scientific research is interested in only the 10% of our DNA that is used for building our bodies, the other 90% they have designated 'junk' DNA. The Russian researchers however, convinced that nature was not wasteful, joined linguists and geneticists in a venture to explore the so called 'junk DNA'.

Their research explains phenomena such as clairvoyance, intuition, spontaneous and remote acts of healing, self-healing, affirmation techniques, unusual light/auras around people, the mind's influence on weather patterns and much more. They found that the genetic code follows the same rules as all human languages. They compared the rules of syntax, semantics and the basic rules of grammar and found that the alkaline of our DNA follow a regular grammar and have set rules just like our languages. The vibrational behaviour of DNA was also explored and experiment proved that living tissue reacted to words and sentences of human language if the proper frequencies are being used proving what esoteric and spiritual teachers have always known, that our body can be programmable by language, words and thought.

The Russian scientists further discuss the process of hyper communication between entirely different areas in the universe, information transmitted outside space and time, and how this is most effective in a state of relaxation. Remote healing, telepathy or 'remote sensing' (intuition) could thus be explained.

I have used the above references to Quantum Mechanics and DNA to allow my characters to appear and disappear in different time lines and dimensions.

Religion

Religion has always been based on unquestioning belief and in all religions there is an understanding of reincarnation and an afterlife.

Individually we all have our beliefs as to the nature of our existence and its limitations. The only certainty we have is that we are going to die, we shed our mortal, physical existence. It could be suggested that we create a belief system in order to comfort ourselves that there is some purpose to our existence?

In the past centuries Science in its quest for proof, answers to everything, has dominated western thought and in doing so questioned our belief systems; we have been displaced from the nature of our emotional and spiritual existence. How does one prove that God exists?

Now with scientific explanations as to the nature of our existence, with the difficulties of measuring this with precision, perhaps it opens a new and refreshing debate as to the nature of belief systems.

Appendix II

Reference: Wikipedia, List of Epidemics

Epidemics and Pandemics with Atleast 1 Million Deaths

Rank	Epidemics/pandemics	Disease	Death toll	Global population lost	Regional population lost	Date	Location
1	Black Death	Bubonic plague	75–200 million	17–54%[Note 1]	30–60% of European population[4]	1346–1353	Europe, Asia, and North Africa
2	Spanish flu	Influenza A/H1N1	17–100 million	1–5.4%[5][6]	–	1918–1920	Worldwide
3	Plague of Justinian	Bubonic plague	15–100 million	7–56%[Note 1]	25–60% of European population[7]	541–549	Europe and West Asia
4	HIV/AIDS global epidemic	HIV/AIDS	36.3 million (as of 2020)	[Note 2]	–	1981–present	Worldwide
5	COVID-19 pandemic	COVID-19	5.7–23.8 million (as of February 1, 2022)[Note 3]	0.07–0.27%[2]	–	2019[Note 4]–present	Worldwide
6	Third plague pandemic	Bubonic plague	12–15 million	[Note 2]	–	1855–1960	Worldwide
7	Cocoliztli epidemic of 1545–1548	Cocoliztli	5–15 million	1–3%[Note 1]	27–80% of Mexican population[13]	1545–1548	Mexico
8	Antonine Plague	Smallpox or measles	5–10 million	3–6%[3]	25–33% of Roman population[14]	165–180 (possibly up to 190)	Roman Empire
9	1520 Mexico smallpox epidemic	Smallpox	5–8 million	1–2%[Note 1]	23–37% of Mexican population[13]	1519–1520	Mexico
10	1918–1922 Russia typhus epidemic	Typhus	2–3 million	0.1–0.16%[6][Note 5]	1–1.6% of Russian population[15]	1918–1922	Russia

11	1957–1958 influenza pandemic	Influenza A/H2N2	1–4 million	0.03–0.1%[2]	–	1957–1958	Worldwide
12	Hong Kong flu	Influenza A/H3N2	1–4 million	0.03–0.1%[2]	–	1968–1969	Worldwide
13	Cocoliztli epidemic of 1576	Cocoliztli	2–2.5 million	0.4–0.5%[3]	50% of Mexican population[13]	1576–1580	Mexico
14	735–737 Japanese smallpox epidemic	Smallpox	2 million	1%[3]	33% of Japanese population[16]	735–737	Japan

Rank	Epidemics/pandemics	Disease	Death toll	Global population lost	Regional population lost	Date	Location
15	1772–1773 Persian Plague	Bubonic plague	2 million	0.2–0.3%[3]	[Note 6]	1772–1773	Persia
16	Naples Plague	Bubonic plague	1.25 million	0.2%[3]	[Note 6]	1656–1658	Southern Italy
17	1846–1860 cholera pandemic	Cholera	1 million+	0.08%[3]	–	1846–1860	Worldwide
18	1629–1631 Italian plague	Bubonic plague	1 million	0.2%[3]	[Note 6]	1629–1631	Italy
19	1889–1890 flu pandemic	Influenza (disputed)[17][18]	1 million	0.07%[3]	–	1889–1890	Worldwide

Footnotes and References

[1] Unravelled after 3000 years, the secrets of the singing mummy; CT scans peer through the burial case and bandages to reveal life of the person hidden inside. (Ref. Fiona Macrae, published 9 and 10th April 2014) X-rays reveal the intricate layers of Egyptian mummies (Ref. Michelle Starr, published 27.05.2014)
See inside the Tomb of a High Powered Egyptian Woman (Ref. Erika Engelhaupt, published 03.02.2018)

[2] Monoatomic gold is a white powder processed from gold. This process is well described by David Hudson's research (The story of David Hudson's discovery of Orme; https://monatomic-orme.com/david-hudson)

[3] Internet: Merkaba translates to 'mer' which means light, 'ka' meaning spirit, and 'ba' meaning body. Essentially a vehicle for the light spirit body which can transport ones spiritual body from one dimension to another.

[4] Lost Book of Enki: Memoirs and Prophecies of an Extraterrestrial God by Zecharia Sitchin. 27 July 2004.

[5] Avyon, not confirmed but sources say it is part of the Lyra Constellation.

[6] Shuruppak is a word taken from the Sumerian dictionary: SHURUPPAK = Land of Utmost Well-Being.

[7] The Albigensian Crusade or the Cathar Crusade (1209–1229)

[8] The Order of the Cloister of Lilith

The Order of the Cloister of Lilith had been created a long time ago to protect the bloodline of a 'designated female' in order that through incarnations she would reach the time of the 'Alignment', the time when Earth would be able to ascend to a higher dimension. The purpose of the Cloister was to keep 'alive' this knowledge until the time came when it would be needed.

Within each generation a male is selected from the designated female's family to become initiated into the 'Cloister of Lilith'. He is given a 'Collar' at the time of initiation. It is the designated female that has to be protected along with the Collar that has been passed down.

The Collar was passed to Maddy instead of a male of the family as the time of the Alignment approached and she would need to become aware of the role she would play. The Order still required a male relative to continue his protective role.

[9] Queen Elizabeth I of England and Ireland (1533–1603)

[10] Downton Abbey: popular BBC TV series.

[11] Mitochondrial DNA and human evolution

Authors: Brigitte Pakendorf, Mark Stoneking

Several unique properties of human mitochondrial DNA (mtDNA), including its high copy number, maternal inheritance, lack of recombination, and high mutation rate, have made it the molecule of choice for studies of human population history and evolution.

[12] Essassani: Internet information, speculative.

Essassani is the home-world of the Sassani race: their planet exists about 500 light years in the direction of the Orion constellation but it is no longer in our frequency band and therefore not detectable by us.

The Sassani ('beings of light') are a successful hybridisation of Zeta and human genes and exist 300–700 years in the future from our current time frame. They possess a combination of the best characteristics of the two races – human and Zeta Reticulan. They have the Zeta's telepathy, longevity, sensitivity, scientific and intellectual capacities as well as humanity's vital, emotional, sexual and physical aspects.

[13] The Isle of Goats

Gavrinis is a small island in the Gulf of Morlihan in Brittany, France – known as the Isle of Goats – Breton word 'gavr' (goat) and 'enez' (island). The Gavrinis Passage Tomb is an ancient burial ground which is thought to have been constructed around 3,500 BC. The site features a stone burial chamber which is covered in a cairn, or stone mound, with a mound of earth packed on top of it. When the tomb was constructed thousands of years ago, the island of Gavrinis was still connected to the mainland.